Out of Time

By Samira Azzam

Translated by Ranya Abdelrahman

Published in 2022 by ArabLit Books. Email: info@arablit.org
www.arablit.org

Translation Copyright © 2022 Ranya Abdelrahman

Out of Time is a work of fiction.

No part of this book may be reproduced in any form, or by any means, without prior permission in writing from the translator or publisher.

ISBN: 9798362585235

	Introduction M Lynx Qualey	vi
	"Out of Time" By Adania Shibli	viii
1	Tears from a Glass Eye	1
2	No Harm Intended	5
3	Lest the Arteries Harden	7
4	Sheikh Mabrouk	11
5	Being a Good Mother	15
6	The Inheritance	18
7	The Aunt's Marriage	20
8	But Until Then	24
9	Pink Curtains	30
10	The Little Things	35
11	A Silken Dream	40
12	On the Road	44
13	From Afar	47
14	Her Story	52
15	Night Visions	57
16	The Ironing Man's Apprentice	60

17	The Bicycle Pump	65
18	I Want Water	68
19	When Wives Fall Ill	72
20	Salt	82
21	Night of Riddance	84
22	The Mad Bell-Ringer	89
23	Everything Was Silenced	92
24	The Rival	96
25	The Roc Flew Over Shahraban	101
26	The Passenger	106
27	Another Year	110
28	Zagharid	115
29	On the Way to Solomon's Pools	119
30	When Hajj Mohammed Sold Out His Hajj	124
31	Because He Loved Them	132

INTRODUCTION

In June of 1967, after watching the shape of her country suddenly change for the second time, with hundreds of thousands more Palestinians expelled from their homes, Samira Azzam destroyed the novel she had been working on. Its title must have seemed particularly tragic in the wake of '67: *Sinai Without Borders*. Two months later, at the age of 39, Azzam went on a road trip with friends. They were outside of al-Ramtha, Syria, when she suffered a heart attack and died.

We had Samira Azzam (1927–1967) for far too few years, and we never got to read what she would do with a novel. Still, she did leave us with five vivid short-story collections, as well as reviews, articles, translations, and countless hours of broadcast radio. Yet after her death, her work fell into a half-shadow, in which she was acknowledged as great, but not quite canonized. In a 2018 article on the Palestinian short story, the critic Faisal Darraj says it plainly: "Azzam has not yet received the accolades she deserves."

There are conflicting theories as to why this happened, but perhaps it's enough to say that Samira Azzam was a short-story writer who died young.

Azzam must have been a passionate writer from a very young age. Raised in a middle-class Christian family in the seaside city of Acre, she began working as a schoolteacher at 16. It was only shortly into her tenure as a teacher when, in her late teens, she started contributing stories and reviews to the newspaper *Filistin* under the pen name "A Girl from the Coast."

Then, at the cusp of 21, everything changed. She, along with hundreds of thousands of other Palestinians, was forced to flee her home. Azzam ended up making a new life in Lebanon, and the life of the refugee is something to which her stories often return. But although a middle-class female narrator sometimes appears in her stories, Azzam's interest was not in self-portraiture, but rather in looking around her, and in imagining the interior lives of a myriad of her fellow Palestinians, from sweaty new graduates to washerwomen to men who made their living reciting poetry at funerals. A topic she returned to again and again was how people dealt with a harsh and rapidly changing world. How did they keep themselves afloat and hold onto their grip on reality? How did their views on morality change, both in how they judged themselves and others? How did the institution of family change, and what about relationships?

Although Azzam was from a middle-class family and worked as a school director, radio broadcaster, author, and translator, she was certainly familiar with how a person's world could be yanked out from beneath them. She brings this deeply felt sympathy to her characters, whose worlds are often transforming around them, sometimes slowly and sometimes all at once.

Azzam's work came to prominence in the 1950s, at a time when Palestinian fiction was still focused on the short story, which—since it could be published in broadsheets and read aloud on the radio—circulated far more widely than the novel. In the 1950s and early '60s, Azzam was an acclaimed and beloved author. She was also an active participant in Beirut's literary scene, which, in the decade before Lebanon's civil war, was in one of its most fertile periods of experimentation.

Although Palestine was the star around which Samira Azzam revolved, only a few of her stories—seven—explicitly mention Palestine or Palestinians. Indeed, some found her work insufficiently political and even insufficiently Palestinian. In her essay on Samira Azzam, Adania Shibli writes about how Azzam's story, "The Clock and the Man," was included in her school curriculum because the censorship board found it harmless. And yet, as Shibli writes, the story "contributed to shaping my consciousness regarding Palestine as no other text I have ever read has done." Nearly all of Azzam's stories are about humans facing some sort of injustice, whether it is economic, social, familial, or the injustice of clocks and borders.

By the 1960s, literary attention was shifting to the novel. In February 1962, writing in *al-Adab*, Azzam reflected on these changes:

> "It seems to me that the Arabic short story is going through difficult times. The reason might not lie in its nature, as much as it does in factors outside of it, including its subjugation to the novel. Writers of the short story have become convinced that writing a novel is the measure of their creativity, especially since short story collections are not heralded by critics the same way novels are: The publication of a story collection goes by without anyone even trying to say a single word about it… And publishing houses hesitate to accept story collections, as if publishing them is a risky venture."

The novel has, if anything, grown into a larger presence, taking up more and more seats at the literary table. A woman writer who produced only short stories in the 1940s, '50s, and '60s is easy to push to the very edges of the table, particularly in a period when we are obsessed with the new, the young and emerging, the published-last-week-and-no-earlier. And yet Samira Azzam's work persists from the margins, much like her vividly imagined characters. And just as her characters are forced to reinvent themselves, the stories are here re-built and re-imagined in a new language, for new readers.

OUT OF TIME

By Adania Shibli

My little watch is the first to sense the change, going into and out of Palestine. On the way there I notice it on my wrist, counting the time down to the second, waiting for the moment when the wheels of the plane touch the runway, and I set it to local time which it counts with an infinite familiarity. Then, as soon as I leave Palestine, my watch advances listlessly, taking its time parting with the local time there, which only vanishes when the plane touches down elsewhere.

It may seem to some that I'm slightly exaggerating what I'm saying about my watch, especially as it is a very tiny watch. People are often amazed that it can tell me the time at all, being so tiny. I myself would have shared their doubts had I not found out about watches and their secret powers, as I did.

It goes back to primary school, during one of the Arabic literature classes. The curriculum back then was, and still is, subject to the approval of the Israeli Censorship Bureau, which allowed teaching texts from various Arab countries, bar Palestine, fearing that they would contain references or even hints that could raise the pupils' awareness of the Palestine Question. Hence, Palestinian literature was considered unlawful, if not taboo, similar to pornography. Except for one text, "The Clock and the Man," a short story by Samira Azzam, which the Censorship Bureau had found "harmless."

OUT OF TIME

The story, published in 1963, is about a young man getting ready to turn in the night before his very first day at work. He sets his alarm clock for four in the morning so as to catch the train in time to get to work. No sooner did the alarm go off the next morning than there came a knocking at his front door. When he opened it, he found an old man in front of him. He had no clue who this man was and he did not get a chance to ask him, because the man turned and walked away, disappearing into the darkness. This was repeated day after day, so that the young man no longer set the alarm. It was only several months later that he discovered who the old man was, after a colleague told him this man went knocking on the doors of all the employees in the company. He would wake them up in order for them not to be late for their trains and meet the same fate as his own son. His son had arrived late at the station one morning, just as the train was leaving. He held onto its door, but his hand betrayed him and he slipped, falling under the wheels of the train.

At first glance, this story might seem simple and safe, especially to the censor's eyes. But it contributed to shaping my consciousness regarding Palestine as no other text I have ever read has done. Were there once Palestinian employees who commuted to work by train? Was there a train station? Was there once a train whistling in Palestine? Was there ever once a normal life in Palestine? So where is it now, and why has it vanished?

The text engraved in my soul a deep yearning for all that had been, including the normal, the banal and the tragic, to such an extent that I could no longer accept the marginalized, minor life to which we've been exiled since 1948, when our existence turned into a "problem."

Against this story and the possible ways of existence it revealed to me, stands my little watch. And my watch is more like that old man in Azzam's story than a Swiss watch that its primary concern is to count time with precision. Rather, just as that old man turned from a human being into a watch in order for life to become bearable, so did my watch decide to turn from a watch into a human being.

So it is not unusual that, in Palestine, my watch often stops moving. It suddenly goes into a coma, unable to count time. On my last visit there, I set it, as always, to local time the minute the plane touched down at Lydd Airport. It was ten-to-two in the afternoon. I headed toward passport control. There weren't many travelers and the line I stood in was proceeding quickly. I handed my passport over to the police officer and she took her time looking at it. Then more time. Suddenly, two men and a woman appeared, a mix of police, security, and secret services. They took me out of the line and began a long process of questioning and searches. Everything proceeded as usual in such situations: an exhaustive interrogation into the smallest details of my life and a thorough search of my luggage. Afterwards, I was led into a room for a body search and, while one woman walked away with my shoes and belt to x-ray them, another stayed behind with my watch, which she held in her palm, contemplating it with great intent and devotion. After a few minutes, she looked at her watch, then back at mine. And again at her watch, then at mine. When the first woman came back with the rest of my belongings, she hurried over to tell her that there was something very strange about my watch. It was not moving. Five minutes had passed according to her watch, whereas according to mine, none had. They called the security chief and my heart started to bang violently in my chest.

I don't know how much time passed before my watch, then I, were cleared of all suspicions and allowed to leave. But I discovered when I reached home that it was nine o'clock in the evening, while my watch was still pointing to ten-to-two in the afternoon. Perhaps my watch was trying to comfort me by making me believe that all that search and delay had lasted zero minutes. That nothing had happened. Or maybe it simply refuses to count the time that is seized from my life, time whose only purpose is to humiliate me and drive me to despair; a suspension of time that is intended for the obstruction of oppression.

Contrary to this malfunctioning in Palestine, my watch has not once stopped outside it. It is never late when counting every second of this other time. In fact, it often moves faster than it should, to a point where it seems to lose track of time altogether. It moves fast as if wanting to shake off this other time from the dial, one second after the other, in order to catch up with the time in Palestine.

In the end, no matter where I am, my little watch leads me out of time, only to comfort me.

Autumn 2006

OUT OF TIME

TEARS FROM A GLASS EYE

His mission comes in three stages. The first starts around six a.m., or a little earlier, while I'm still busy hanging up the morning papers on the wooden stand. He comes over, biting into a knafeh sandwich, sugar syrup dripping down his chin, and asks about the news. I insist on cracking a joke that was already stale ten years ago, pointing at the red headlines and saying, "Read it yourself! You can read, can't you? But pay the quarter before you touch a single one of those papers." He laughs, the remains of the sandwich showing through his yellowed teeth, and says, "If I read one word outside the column, I'll pay whatever you want."

When something becomes a habit, you stop reacting to it. That is, I don't get angry the way I used to, ten years ago, and I'm no longer disgusted by the way he looks, his cheeks stuffed with food. Without getting too worked up, I open up the two big dailies and point to the obituaries. "Go ahead and read, but don't touch anything with your filthy hands."

Not wasting a moment, he takes out an old stub of a pen and writes down the names of the deceased, leaving out only the names of the old women.

Actually, I don't want to gloss over that last part. It was months before I thought to ask him how he could tell which names belonged to old women. He laughed his sleazy laugh and said, "Come on, Ustaz, every woman who's done all her religious duties must be old. And people don't pay a thing for elegies of old women, so I've got no business with them."

If there was a photo at the top of the obituary, he would stare at it, goggle-eyed, and then his sleazy smile would return, spreading across his face. "A young one... a young one...," he'd say. "The daaliyyah poem will be perfect. It's been tucked away for a month now. This photo should earn me at least twenty liras, or fifty if I manage to cry. Do you think the name will fit, Ustaz? Never mind, we'll think about that later—now, open that other paper for me."

I open it, and he copies down more names. Then he puts the list into his pocket, saying, "And now we're off to ask for addresses and sort through the poems. We'll need four: one of the poems will work for two of them. We just need to come up with something for that old man with the strange name. As for the fourth, I've got a poem that fits so well, it's as if it was written for him!"

After that, he leaves me, and this is where the second stage begins. For him, it's the hardest part. He might have to roam all four corners of the city, stopping in front of every flyer covered in black ink that's been stuck on a wall or a lamppost, to read the dead person's full details. If it's an old flyer, he pulls it off so he won't waste time checking it again the next day, a task for which, in his opinion, he deserves to be rewarded by the city. Otherwise, what kind of state would the walls be in, if the flyers piled up, one on top of the other?

And if I said, "You pull them off the wall to throw them on the ground?"

He'd answer, "God forbid! The names of the dead are sacred! I gather them up in a stack and toss them into the nearest bin. Come on, Ustaz, we've seen charity from most of them, and we still have a little dignity left, you know."

I study his expression for any trace of dignity, and my gaze gets lost in the lines, which barely move when he laughs or cries. In the folds, little white hairs have sprouted, which he won't shave all the way off—a well-trimmed beard isn't part of the grieving look. His features hunch under a shabby tarboush, its tassel having lost most of its threads. This tarboush has a mission not tasked to every one of its kind: right beneath it, on the sweat-drenched surface of his bald spot, he places the chosen poem, so his fingers won't pick the wrong one from amongst four or five others. He's afraid he might get the names mixed up: "We got it wrong once," he told me, and I tried to catch his meaning through the sound of his breathy laughter, "and… I read a man's poem for a woman. I'll never forgive myself for that one. It got me thrown out of the dead woman's house and cost me the payment I was expecting, plus the ten piasters to get there and back by tram, not to mention that I had to climb ninety stairs! All I got from her family was a Bafra cigarette, which fell out of my hand when I pulled myself free from the idiot who was pushing me. Earning my daily bread isn't easy!"

I feel a bit of schadenfreude as I tell him it serves him right, since he's picked the lowest way to earn his living. He frowns, and I see a flash of pain clouding his faded eyes. "Each of us has his calling."

If he's still doing his rounds, he'll definitely be in front of a mosque or church by now. From the breadth of the family's preparations, he gets a measure of the deceased's place in society and he can tell, with amazing intuition, exactly how much he can expect to make. I see him again, when the daytime sun has grown vicious, sitting in the shade on an ancient staircase, digging multiple bits of paper out of the pockets of his green-black suit. With his whittled-down pen, he crosses out names and writes one in place of another. Dead people of every ilk, faith, and age have their virtues distilled into three or four verses, not one of which makes any sense, unless it was stolen from somewhere. It didn't matter, though—or that's what he says. The grieving don't understand anyway; after a day filled with a tumult of emotion, their brains have stopped working entirely.

Actually, from where I sit—and without needing to see him in action more than four or five times—I can tell exactly how he is at a funeral. He might be the only actor in the world who plays a single role for his entire lifetime. At more than one show a night, his bottom lip is called on to quickly start trembling, and then everything about him seems to take on the same quivering motion: his sleeves and his legs, his saggy pants and the button on his tarboush, which has slipped down to the middle of his forehead. He lingers for a few minutes, his shaking unabated. And then, after the sweat has gathered in big drops under his tarboush, he pulls it off, takes a sheet of paper from inside it, and goes over to where the home's owners are seated. He begins to read, in a defeated voice that is utterly toneless except when he speaks the name of the deceased. The elegy is personal, very personal: he doesn't care if the name is far removed from its context; he knows how to squeeze it in. When he gets to the end, he wipes the sweat off his forehead and takes two steps forward, clasping the hand of the person closest to the deceased in both of his. By now, a couple of notes have been pressed into his hand, and he nimbly magics them away and takes himself off to his chair, where he allows himself a cigarette. Snatching one from the nearest table, he sniffs the tobacco through its unfiltered tip, keeping it unlit so that, if it's imported, he can exchange it for two locals the next day.

Now, if someone were to think this was just easy money, then they would be selling the man short in any number of ways. Some people can't be coaxed into mourning their dearly departed with worn-out words, sucked dry of all meaning. But our shameless friend has skin so thick, no amount of pummeling can penetrate it. Regardless of how the mourners pull at his sleeve, having heard his poem at twenty other funerals, he won't stop. And however hard they try to push him out, he is perfectly capable of repeating his theatrical entrance a few minutes later. So shelling out was the price of saving themselves from a situation that would disturb their mourning and insult the dignity of the deceased. Some people would offer him the money before he had finished reciting the first verse, but he would refuse to cut his reading short—it wasn't just the money that breathed strength into his legs, which were plagued every winter by rheumatism. If they forced him to stop, he would weep and tremble even harder as his fingers felt their way into his pocket.

I don't want to accuse him of setting his sights on me, or to say his blade touched my throat on purpose. I was in my bookshop, bent over some stamp collections with my tweezers, sorting them into little envelopes, when the phone rang. It was the kind of ringing that brings on a feeling of dread and a reluctance to make it stop by picking up the receiver. How could he of all people be dead? And how? Scattered to dust with the remains of a burning plane? I felt my nails dig into the flesh of my palms as I trod in circles like a bull around a waterwheel, until my brother stopped by and pulled me outside, then locked the store and dropped the keys into my pocket.

I used to love that cousin of mine. He was my guide to the city at night, and, without him, stepping outside the confines of my store turned me into a child lost in the market. The news wasn't in any newspapers or on any posters. Instead, it was announced on all the radio stations and was on the lips of hundreds of people. These were the sort of people who, for a few short hours, would succumb to a philosophizing that put them in the mood of pious humility: if they weren't the victims, then they needed, at least, to be witnesses. By evening, my uncle's house was crowded with callers, and I saw faces I don't remember having seen anywhere before. The air was thick with bitterness and pain, and I had an arm around my uncle's shoulders, bracing him so he could endure his manly sorrows without collapsing like a tattered rag. Just then, I saw our friend cutting through the crowd. He looked like a wind-up toy as he came in, having been overtaken by a trembling that ran from the button of his tarboush, to his lips, to his sleeves, and down through his pant legs. He sat on a chair, given up to him by a boy from the family, and the plastic contours of his face went through their tragic contortions as sweat began to gather in droplets on his forehead. As he reached out, pulled off his tarboush, and took out the sheet of paper, my arm went slack around my uncle's shoulder and my hands began to clench and unclench.

I was suddenly on full alert, itching to stand up, incensed by a grief that, in an instant, had turned to rage. I stood and took a single step, then bumped into the table. He was already standing—perhaps he hadn't noticed me before because, as soon as he saw me, the trembling in his body stopped, his features froze, and a fleeting gleam flashed through his gummy eyes. Reaching unhurriedly into his pocket for a handkerchief, he dried his head with it and fixed his tarboush back in place. He came up to us then, with a bit of purpose in his stride, and kissed me, shook my uncle's hand, and left.

NO HARM INTENDED

In the confectionery store we run, we've been following the same system ever since our father put us to work there: dividing the store's duties between us, assigning some of us to sales, others to accounting. As for my father, he never stayed in one place; he did everything and nothing at the same time.

If he caught a hint of reluctance or aversion in us as we served someone, he would say, "Be nice to people, offer them a little of whatever they see in front of them. Giving a piece here or there won't do any harm, and a gesture like that will charm most people into making up their minds, even if they'd been hesitating."

We took his advice, and we saw that it worked. But, to be fair, only a few customers agreed to taste the sweets, and almost none of these were men. Not too fussy for the most part, the men would ask by name for the item their wives had told them to buy. As for the women, they were something else entirely. One of them would spend ages deliberating and comparing, accepting with a smile everything we offered to taste and then, as we arranged the pieces in their cardboard boxes, she would be "on our backs," as they say, making sure everything was done just so.

Still, there were exceptions among the men, and one of these was a man who used to visit us twice a week. Before coming in, he would stand at the door for a while with his hands knotted behind his back, and then he'd break into a smile that revealed his missing front teeth. As he entered the store, his eyes would dart between the piles of toffees and sweets, and my brother and I would exchange a meaningful smile that I don't think the man ever noticed. He would ask about our new products, and, keeping straight faces, we would wax lyrical about their excellence. With rapt eyes, his mouth watering, he would listen in silence punctuated with an occasional, "I see, I see." Feeling sorry for him by this point, we would give him a piece, which he'd place between his teeth, sucking on it and rolling it to the left or right where he still had teeth to rely on, teeth he didn't have at the front of his mouth. When he was done, he'd wipe his mouth with the back of his hand, saying, "It's sweet, too sweet. I wish it had less sugar in it," or, "You can smell the eggs in it, I don't like that." We'd laugh, as we too would say, "I see, I see."

We knew he never bought anything, and that he had nothing in his pocket to buy with, but he couldn't resist his childish love of sweets. Coming to the shop was a way for him to taste a slice of cake, or one of the thousands of stacked-up pieces of candy. When we grumbled about it, my father would chide us: "Don't deny him this small pleasure, maybe it's the only one he has in his life. Let him be."

One morning, the old man arrived when the shop was jam-packed with customers buying sweets for Eid in huge amounts, totally unlike on regular days. I raised an indignant hand when he came in, earning myself a disapproving look from my father. Before the old man could open his mouth, my father had reached toward the wrapped boxes we had prepared to send out as gifts to our regular customers, picking one up and offering it to him, saying, "This is for you, it's for Eid." And when the man hesitated, my father began to coax him, "It's a present, a present. Aren't you a regular here? Go on, take it."

The man was clearly embarrassed—the veins in his neck dilated slightly and a hint of redness crept into his face—but he neither picked up the box nor left. Instead, he put it aside, saying, "I want something else." He paused, then continued with a long list of items: "That box of chocolates there, the big one, and… and, two dozen coconut cookies, and a kilo—are you writing this down, young lady? Write it down so you don't forget. No, make it two kilos of this toffee, and… and this candied citron, my family loves it. Put them all into one bundle along with the gift and make up my bill. I'll stop by to pick them up on my way home, and I'll pay you… Yes, I'll pay you…"

After saying this, he swung around, almost bumping into an old woman and a child in his haste. He left without so much as a farewell glance at the storefront, keeping his gaze averted until he reached a string of shops in which he seemed to have no interest.

Do I need to say that we didn't bother to prepare the items and wrap them? And that we didn't believe—even if we had gotten them ready—that he would stop back to pick them up? But what really pained us was that he had left behind the box we'd given him as a gift, and that, after that morning, we never saw his face again.

LEST THE ARTERIES HARDEN

The evening grew dark, and a heavy gray sky pressed down on the city, where small colored lights couldn't hold on to the daylight. Drizzling rain had wrapped them in mist, soaking up their glow until they were as faint as nightlights, glimmering red or green. He stood in front of the hotel where the company put passengers on overnight transit, looking up and down the road. He didn't want to ask the information-desk employee—who seemed ready to provide every kind of service—or get a tour guide, so he decided to let chance cast him into any one of the places where lights glowed dimly under the wintry evening sky.

He chose to turn right and started to walk; the drizzle was bearable, so he didn't hurry. He would have kept on walking until he was tired and then turned into the nearest establishment, but the rain grew steadily stronger and, a minute later, water was pouring down from above and welling up from under the sidewalks. Cars started honking more impatiently as they navigated the narrow lanes, barely two meters wide, and when passersby began to push past him, he decided to cut his journey short. He looked around, trying to find a signboard indicating shelter. Eventually, a waiter carrying a towel saved him from searching any longer. The man waved for him to come in, so he did.

The place was empty. It was cold, too, and there was no soft lighting and no music. This was a place whose customers didn't turn to gimmicks for their drinking. He might have been hoping for a bit of that, but at least the bartender was friendly—he needed someone who would smile back at him.

"Your place is empty."

"It's only six. You're starting early."

"I'm a stranger here."

"And it shows."

The bartender smiled at him and gratefully accepted a cigarette but refused his offer to buy him a drink. Not finding anything else to say, he picked up a folded newspaper from the bar. The paper was old, so he skipped the first page and passed time with the crime and entertainment sections. When he'd finished with all the trivial news, he folded the paper with a sigh and ordered another drink, then turned his chair and took a good look around him.

The rain had stopped and traffic thinned. The narrow road, washed by the downpour, seemed to shine, reflecting dim yellow lights off its surface. And the evening seemed to get kinder and friendlier when people started coming into the bar. They greeted the bartender from across the room as they rubbed their hands together and nodded hellos to each other, then plopped down at a table or tipped back their heads to order, saying things that made no sense to him.

One man sat down and said, "Let's get started! One to keep—" Then he snatched up the cognac the waiter handed him, drinking half of it in one go.

A second man said something similar but got a different drink. When he heard the same phrase from a third person, he turned to the bartender. "What are they saying?"

"Oh, them?" He laughed, then collected his features into a more serious expression. "Will you be here long?"

"I've got nothing else to do, might as well stay another hour."

"Good. She should be here in an hour, and the story won't stand on its own without her."

And he laughed again.

Less than half an hour later, the bartender came up behind him and shook him. "She's here. That's her."

He looked toward the door and saw an old woman: weak, scraggy, and unkempt, with silver hair and restless eyes. "What's wrong with her?"

"Hold on and I'll explain. Come here and look out the window. See that room there, above the warehouses?"

"Yes."

"That's her home... It's the home where she's lived since forever, or at least since I've been working here these past twenty-five years. I'm ancient, ancient. When I started work at this place, my son Hanna hadn't been born yet, and Hanna's a grown man now, and married."

"Fine, but what's your business with her?" he asked, now suddenly alert, since he'd found something to drive off the drowsy monotony.

"Nothing, nothing. She used to have a husband, a stocky old guy who carried a stick. Every day, they'd come down—him leaning on his stick, her leaning on him and his stick. They'd sit by the wall at that old coffeehouse over there. Come, put your head out a little and you'll see it from the window. Anyway, that's what they'd do if the day was clear. If it rained, well, they'd sit at home in their window seat. And they wouldn't budge until it got dark.

"Nobody visited them, and they visited nobody. They were cut from the family tree. And they lived... I don't know how they lived, but the grocer's boy was the only one who—two or three times a week—went up the outside staircase that led to their room.

"Then one day, we stopped seeing the old man sitting like a statue by the window or coming down the stairs on his way to the coffeehouse. We only saw the woman. She'd peek out, then disappear—she never braved the staircase. But one day mid-morning, I was hanging my jacket on this hook here, when I turned and saw her standing right behind me. She seemed lost. Embarrassed.

"'My husband's sick,' she said, 'and the doctor, the doctor himself, advised him to drink a little whiskey. One tablespoon with or without tea. He's got clogged arteries. But he doesn't drink... He might resist, but I'll try. Would you sell me a bottle? How much do you want for it?'

"When I handed her the bottle and told her the price, she hesitated. 'That much? My God, how people waste their money! We see you from our window. We see how your customers drink until they're staggering. In any case, here—take it, take it, necessity makes its own rules...' And she gave me the money from a black bag, took the bottle, and left.

"The old man didn't die for another year—I carried his coffin myself with five others, including the priest. In all that time, she never bought another bottle. Then a week after he died, she brought the bottle back and asked to return it because—and she swore this was true—the bottle was just as it had been, unopened. 'My husband, God rest his soul, stubbornly refused to taste a single drop, even though—' and here her tears began to fall '—he obeyed all the doctor's instructions. But nothing could convince him to drink even a single spoonful with a cup of tea.'

"I looked at the bottle and didn't doubt the woman was telling the truth. It was the same bottle I'd sold her a year before. I wondered if it was fair for me to take something back I'd sold a year ago, and then, moved by her tears, I said—and of course I only meant it as a joke—'Why don't you drink it?' Her face went as red as a boiled beetroot and she snapped back at me, 'Are you making fun of me? Give it here if you won't let me return it.'

"I'd meant to give back her money and take the bottle, but she snatched it and ran across the street, then up the stairs to her house. I felt bad for her. I honestly didn't mean to make fun of her. It was just a joke, and I don't know why she took it so hard."

At this point, one of the customers clapped his hands, and he heard the same words, "One to keep—" Then the bartender excused himself. He picked up a small bottle of arak, a glass, and a small bowl of seeds. He handed them to the waiter, and then returned to their conversation.

"Where were we? Oh, yeah, I definitely wasn't making fun of her. But you have to hear what happened next. The woman stayed away for a month, or maybe longer, and then one morning she came in. She looked thin and tired out, and she glanced around anxiously as she walked up to me, saying, 'I want another bottle. This one's finished. Take it, if it's any use to you empty. If my husband had drunk, he wouldn't have died from clogged arteries. That's what the doctor said. If only he'd agreed to drink…' Then she started to cry, and I didn't know how to comfort her. I gave her the bottle, and she stuffed it into a bag and whispered to me before she stepped out, 'Don't you tell anyone about this.'

"She started buying a bottle every two weeks, then every week, then every day or so, until she had nothing left to buy with. She said some brother of her husband's who lived abroad used to send them money, but he cut that off after his brother died. So she started selling her furniture, one piece after another, until the only thing left in her room was the bed she slept on. Then she sold that, too, and kept the mattress. I don't know if she's got anything to sleep on now. She started coming to me, begging for a drink, and I'd give her one, but one glass wasn't enough anymore, so she started in on the customers. She won't accept a drink until she tells her story. And she can tell it a hundred times to any one of them. She goes up to them and says, 'You drink, that's why you're not going to die from clogged arteries like my husband. And I drink, because I don't want to die like that either. I never tasted a drop before he died, just ask, ask Abu Hanna.' And she looks to me for help.

"And they give to her, they willingly offer her drinks. No one brushes her off and they're even more generous when they're drunk. She's become part of this bar, and they miss her if she's away, even for just one night, and when they call out their orders, they say, 'One to keep—'. You get what they mean, right? '—to keep the arteries from clogging.'"

The old woman stared out at everyone and smiled. Seeing that he was the only stranger, she singled him out with a longer gaze, and then she came forward to inspect him from up close. She had the look of an addict, and behind that face was silence. Her face told a story of loneliness—so vicious it was almost inhuman—and when he saw she was about to open her mouth to tell her story, he leapt in first, asking, "Would you like a drink? It keeps the arteries from clogging."

"Oh, you're like me. You know it, too," she said with a little cheer, her lips spreading away from an ancient, toothless mouth. "Yes, I'll have one…"

The bartender finished: "…to keep the arteries from clogging."

SHEIKH MABROUK

My neighbor looked in on me with his ancient face and said, "Isn't it odd that we haven't seen Sheikh Mabrouk in days?"

"I've missed him, too," I said, without lifting my scissors from where I was at work on a customer's hair. "I don't know what's happened to him. Maybe he's sick."

"Strange, I thought Sheikh Mabrouk didn't get sick—"

"Well, why wouldn't he? Isn't he human, just like you and me?"

"Yes, but—"

"But what?"

My neighbor couldn't find anything to say, so he turned and left, leaving me to think about Sheikh Mabrouk, who hadn't been in to visit us lately. We weren't used to him not showing up because, for the past ten years, he had stopped by every day without fail, never missing a visit, except on holidays and feast days.

There were many strange things about Sheikh Mabrouk. I had known him since I'd started on as an apprentice at the barber's shop, which, as things go, I later came to manage. I used to watch him with great interest, staring at his tall, slender frame; his handsome, bearded face; and the long string of black prayer beads that dangled from his right hand, my eyes moving from his faded turban to his old jilbab—which was always spotless—and down to the leather slippers in which he nimbly walked around.

In the beginning, I didn't know what lay behind his daily visits, as he neither sat down nor lingered. He'd come in and call out a soft greeting, and then my boss's hand would reach out to give him a single piaster, which he tossed into his pocket before leaving us to visit our neighbor. From there, he would move in turn along the long line of barber shops, upholsterers, and second-hand clothes stores, collecting piasters from each on his way. I was confused about who Sheikh Mabrouk truly was, which made me curious: Was he a beggar? No, he had neither the look nor the personality of beggars, nor any of the wiles they used to gain sympathy and coax charity. There was a perpetual cleanliness about him, and a sense of pride that bridled his tongue from uttering a word of thanks in anything but the quietest voice.

And why did they call him "the sheikh"? There were self-styled sheikhs aplenty, but he wasn't like them, either. Those other sheikhs, in my experience, would sit down and recite what they could from the Quran, and then they'd drink a cup or two of coffee and, on top of that, take what charity they could get, praying that every piaster given would be returned in multiples to its giver, and that God would magnify the giver's wealth so he could give generously. No, in spite of the turban and the title, Sheikh Mabrouk wasn't one of them. His general appearance was closest to that of the Moroccans whose trade was in fortune-telling, among other things. So why did the man persist with his daily visits? And why did my boss and our neighbors so willingly give him their coins?

I was too shy to ask my boss, even though I should have known that gossip was essential to our trade, and then I wouldn't have been shy or kept back my question. One day, I drummed up my courage. My boss said, "Wallah my son, I don't know what to say. We believe this man is a harbinger of baraka: whenever he visits, blessings and good fortune descend on the shop. We named him Mabrouk, the blessed one, so his old name was lost. It might have been Mohammed, or Ali, or Khamis—but anyway, we ended up calling him Mabrouk. As for the 'sheikh,' well, it's a good finishing touch for the robe, the turban, and the prayer beads.

"He never asks for anything, never imposes: If we give, he takes, and if we hold back, he leaves without a hint of blame. His face has a look of strange contentment, as if all he needs from the world is a bite of food and the courtyard of a mosque to shelter in when nighttime falls."

"Doesn't he have a wife and children?" I asked, intrigued.

The boss boomed out a laugh that shook the veins in his neck. "A wife?" he said. "Sheikh Mabrouk with a wife? The same man who looks down, avoiding your gaze if you so much as mention women in front of him? No son, that man has given up his worldly pleasures in return for the hereafter." He fell silent when a customer came in and flung himself down on the crudely made chair, surrendering his head to the scissors and opening his ears wide to the boss's stories.

I continued to work for several more years at the barber's shop—or the 'Sit Back and Enjoy Salon,' as the owner called it—and I don't recall a single day when Sheikh Mabrouk didn't come by, except for the days we were closed.

I used to look forward to his visits. He would come in, greet us, collect his money, and then leave without a care in the world, as he had done ever since I started out in the trade as a youngster, until the management of the Sit Back and Enjoy Salon fell to me after my boss died.

So it wasn't surprising that I missed Sheikh Mabrouk, or that I was a bit worried when he stayed away for two whole weeks. But after that, he came back. He walked in one afternoon, greeted us, and walked up to me. I held out the usual piaster, but he looked at me with a confused smile that I had seldom seen on his face and said, "No, I didn't come here for that... no more handouts."

I didn't understand what he meant; I'd never before heard him say so many words at once. So I said, "We haven't seen you for days."

"I was busy," he said, then spoke again in a different tone. "Can you shave off my beard?"

"Shave off your beard?"

"Yes, my beard. They want me clean-shaven like the effendis." He laughed, and I thought his laugh came from deep in his belly.

"Who are they? Who are you talking about?"

"There's a woman, you see. I'm going to marry her."

"You're getting married, Sheikh Mabrouk? For real?"

He smiled, revealing two rows of white teeth. "It was meant to be," he said.

I stood there, staring at his face, not believing my eyes and ears—I thought the man must be raving. "You don't believe me, Hassan," he said, encouragingly. "Perhaps you think I'm mad?"

"Absolutely. Are you joking, Sheikh Mabrouk?"

"No I'm not, I swear. I am getting married."

"To whom?"

"To a woman you don't know. As for me, I've known her a long time. I fell in love with her when she was a young girl and wanted to marry her back then, but her father refused and gave her to his brother's son. His rejection came as a shock, and I couldn't bear it, so I began to wander aimlessly, like a tramp. I felt like a man with no connection to people or life, so I lived as you knew me." Mabrouk stopped talking for a moment, then moistened his lips with his tongue and said, "I thought I'd forgotten her, and that my love for her had died in my heart, until I saw her a month ago, after hearing that her husband had died and left her with a young daughter. And then, Hassan, I realized that I still loved her, and that it was the same love, the only love that's ever lived inside me. I proposed as soon as I crossed her threshold. And she accepted, of course, because under my protection, she'll be kept safe from ending up on the streets. I must get a job now, since I'm going to be responsible for a family. And that's the whole story, my friend. Why aren't you cutting off my beard? How am I supposed to work with this on my face?"

"Well, I'll be—!" I said, unable to decide whether to believe my eyes and ears. Saying nothing more, I picked up the razor, and Sheikh Mabrouk's beard was soon scattered across the floor in front of me, as black as the feathers on a crow.

And, as I removed his beard, I felt I was wiping the myth off of him. The myth of baraka.

BEING A GOOD MOTHER

She went home with dragging steps and found herself the focus of her two sons' attention, their eyes full of questions.

"Who was that man, Mama?"

Lowering her eyes, Nabiha took each of them by the hand and led them to the nearest seat, then tenderly stroked their hair. But they kept looking at her with their father's inquiring eyes, unable to bear any sense of mystery.

What could she possibly say? Should she tell them that the generous man—who never showed up without a bunch of flowers in his right hand, and candy and other gifts for the children in his left—had proposed to marry her and become a father to them? No, she'd say nothing of the kind. The little ones wouldn't understand; they would just shake their heads in confusion and run off to play with their toys, leaving her to think about what this conflict had done to her. They were too young to have noticed that a battle was raging in their mother's conscience, from which she had emerged victorious.

But had she really won? What about her youth, which she had callously ignored? And the whispers she had firmly silenced, and the promise she had refused to hear? Could she call all that a triumph and a victory?

If there was any victory to be found from clinging to her own contrived logic and the values she had adopted, then why hadn't it stilled her throbbing heart, or calmed her restless soul?

She was young. Only a few days had passed since she'd shaken off her twenty-ninth year. And she was beautiful. Grief had not been as cruel as it can be, and her face was still gentle and attractive. And she was weak, and above all a woman—in her experience, life was a scary journey that called for a companion.

Caught up in defending her logic, she had ignored all this, stuffing it into a frozen corner of her heart, shrouding it in denial, so she could wear the robes of a noble martyr. Some victory—it was a victory that reeked of defeat!

Our friend let out a sigh and went back to tenderly stroking her children's hair. How selfish I am! How could I have allowed my youth to make demands, and my spirit to be resentful, when I don't belong to myself as much as I belong to these two little ones?

I am their mother and their father... But why hadn't she said that she was loyal to the memory of her dead husband?

Loyalty...

She felt the word emerging from her thoughts, cold to the touch and faint in her ear. That word—which had once been a chain that kept the smile from her lips and bound her tight to her husband's grave, so that all she inhaled of the world was the scent of memories. So how had the chain grown loose, and that word become swathed in ice?

If this generous man had proposed to her in the years that followed her husband's death, she would have turned away from him with a dismissive wave, only to stare at the large picture of her husband that hung on the wall, saying, "How could I love again, after him?"

But eight long years of arid solitude had taught her to believe that the soul is like a plant, always seeking warm rays, refreshing drinks, and ample shade.

Yes, it was hard for her to boast of her loyalty now, and to hold it up as the sole reason she refused to venture again into the battle of life. After all, she was only human.

But she was also the mother of two little ones, and if she clung to her position, it was for their sake: she was driven by a mother's tender love.

She and her two brothers had also tasted the bitterness of losing their father young. But it had become true bitterness only when her mother remarried.

She couldn't blame her mother. She had been young, too, with no one to take her hand and help her raise her large family. And the man who'd proposed had been prominent and distinguished. He'd tempted her with prestige and position, drowning her in promises until she married him, only for her children to suffer, and for her to suffer on their behalf. She discovered that her husband's heart was too small for her, his personality too weak to be kind, and his hand too miserly to be generous with children who were not his own. He made her life a burning red hell, filling it with never-ending torment. He had children with his dead wife, and he began to accuse Nabiha's mother of favoring her sons and daughter over his household and his offspring. So she was forced to neglect her own flesh and blood to avoid his hateful words.

Her husband was a boorish dictator, and his every command had to be instantly obeyed. He wanted the house kept as quiet as the houses of God, and woe betide any child who was tempted to be noisy by a new toy. Their stepfather's punishment felt second only to being held to account by the two angels of the grave.

Could she ever forget his ranting and raving, and the total disdain in his voice as he mocked her brothers, calling them names? Or the day he had grabbed her elder brother by the scruff of the neck and laid into him with a thick stick because he'd broken a branch in the garden? The brute had paralyzed her mother's hands when he grabbed everything her children's father had left them. After that, he began to argue with her, claiming there was no need to pay for their education.

Yes. She remembered all of it. And she saw yesterday's ghost threatening her—threatening her tomorrows and the tomorrows of her children.

She had lived, miserable and downcast, until she was married. And her marriage had been shorter than a summer night's dream.

Fate had put her in the same role as her mother. And her two little ones now drank from the same cup of deprivation that she and her brothers had drunk from when they were young, now that her husband's death had left her to a new bout of misery. At first, she had lost all faith in life and death and in the Power that played so carelessly with people's destinies. And she had locked herself away from the world with a crazed, single-minded resolution to die. The only thing that forced her back from her madness and blasphemy had been those two children. In them, she saw an extension of her husband's life, the man she had loved with every fiber of her being.

And when she stared into their eyes, she caught a glimpse of his spirit sending her comfort and encouragement, wrapped in humility. So she swore to massage away their pain with a tender hand, and to grow a flower in the desert of her life: she would press on with her mission of sacrifice until the end. For years, she had gently and patiently turned suitors away, until that man appeared on her horizon, and she saw something in him that was different from the rest. She found kindness in him, and understanding and empathy—but she gently refused him, like she'd done with all the others, because she had vowed to see her stepfather's face on all men.

That was her decision, and the matter was over and done with. So there was no point in her thinking about it now. She was, and would always be... a mother.

THE INHERITANCE

We have to confess that Abu Naseef's family was impatient for him to die. And perhaps the unfortunate man, determined to spite them, had chosen to drag out the agony of his dying until it went on for so long that we grew tired of it. We were his neighbors, and we were not impatient for him to die, nor did we expect to gain anything—neither from his life nor from his death.

He lived on the floor above us with his plump, kind-hearted wife. He had no children, as he was infertile, but even though there was no son named Naseef, "Abu Naseef" suited him well. The name belonged to him alone, as we had never heard anyone call his wife "Umm Naseef." Ever since we'd moved into the building, we had known that our neighbor suffered from numerous aches and pains that sometimes stopped him from going out to his store, which was across the road from our house and his. On those occasions, he would simply send his wife to manage the store in his place, along with a relative of hers who worked as an errand boy. If they were uncertain about anything, they would ask Abu Naseef for advice from across the balcony.

Now, if you'd seen what we saw when people found out the man's illness had worsened, you would have known that the impatience of those who would benefit from his death wasn't hidden, and that they didn't even bother to coat it in any sort of hypocrisy. They had designs on his shop, fed by his lack of an heir. They thought it was too much for his wife to gain possession of the store and its contents, and they denied her right to it, even though she had cared for her husband for many long years, during which she'd never once heard him say, "Thank God for my good health."

The news Abu Naseef's family had heard about the will he made during his final days was neither here nor there: it could be challenged on the grounds that the man had been ill when he wrote it and not of sound mind. So they camped out in front of the store, afraid that the wife would move some of the merchandise out behind their backs. They took shifts to guard it. Every day, as soon as morning came, a short, bald, ugly brother of Abu Naseef's would arrive, and he wouldn't leave until an elderly sister of his—

or another, even older sister—took over his shift.

Sometimes the three of them would stand guard together, and they would brazenly visit their dying brother before taking up their positions. There was another spot, on the opposite sidewalk, where some of the wife's family stood; they were afraid their brother-in-law would suddenly die, and that, in one fell swoop, their sister would lose both husband and store.

But Abu Naseef dug in his heels and wouldn't die, tormenting them and leaving them exhausted. We would watch all this from our windows until, after much of the same, the novelty wore off and we went about our business, having lost all interest. But that didn't stop us from noticing, in passing, that the sentry point was unmanned for two days, which naturally piqued our curiosity. We asked around and were told that the ugly bald man had been overcome by a sudden gallantry, and that he had stopped trying to crowd in on his sister-in-law's inheritance. He had convinced his sisters and their husbands that there was something sordid about their behavior and that people wouldn't approve of it: having suffered as she had through their brother's illness, the woman had a right to enjoy some of his wealth when he died, instead of being forced to go begging.

His actions took on immense proportions in the eyes of the neighbors: he no longer looked ugly after chivalry had lent him some respectability and made him taller by a handspan, or even two. And they no longer came up with those hateful explanations for his visits to his brother, suspecting him of being opportunistic. After all, people are softhearted and easily charmed by any sort of heroic gesture.

And then one morning the man died. The wife was filled with grief and tore her dress, and the brothers and sisters wept tears that bore not a hint of hypocrisy. But all of that was over and done within less than a week, when the wife found herself obliged to go back to the store, having neglected it for a long time.

Life ambled on in our good neighborhood; the story disappeared into the past and no one remembered it anymore. The wife sat on her chair at the store, running it with her sweet tongue and her kind, simple smile. Everything relaxed back to normal until there came a day when we found the store closed. We went back to wondering about it, especially since all the windows of the house upstairs were also closed. It wasn't long before we saw our plump, kind-hearted neighbor climbing the stairs one evening. She was hanging onto a man's arm.

"He married her!"

And so it was that, within minutes, people had spread the news, although without tearing the wife apart.

As for him, in their eyes he went back to being an ugly bald man who couldn't keep his hands off his dead brother's property... including his wife!

THE AUNT'S MARRIAGE

It was only natural, since Umm Youssef was visiting, for us to loosen our tongues and delve more freely than usual into the affairs of neighbors, both near and far. Umm Youssef is a news machine, you see, and no one could deny her unstinting efforts to gather information from every inch of our neighborhood. So, naturally, every time she saw you, she'd have a new piece of gossip to share—or perhaps an old one. She might know things about you that you don't know yourself, and some of her revelations might surprise you. What's more, Umm Youssef's knowledge rose above any ifs or buts: she was always sure of her facts.

She sucked greedily on her hand-rolled cigarette, then took a slurp of her coffee and said, "It's going to be a wedding fit for a king—may others be equally blessed. Thing is, Umm Shawqy wants to keep everyone talking about her daughter's wedding: the best tailors in town for the bride's dresses, the most expensive wood for the furniture. And then there's the perfumes, the flowers, the linens—I could go on. And what's to stop her doing all this and more? Let's hope poor Najia's savings survive her niece's big day, and God rest her husband Masoud's soul. It's as if Abu Shawqy, and his children after him, were destined to inherit Masoud's thousands—his thousands of thousands—and to feast on his riches at no cost to themselves except to spout endless prayers for his soul, all lies and for show. Well, talk is cheap! You'd think butter wouldn't melt in that Umm Shawqy's mouth, but I know what she's really like."

When Umm Youssef's tongue stilled for a moment—she was gulping down the final sip of her coffee—my mother asked, "Hasn't Najia had any suitors since her husband died?"

Umm Youssef opened her eyes until they were as round as a cat's. "What a question! How simple are you, woman? Is there a man alive who wouldn't want to get his hands on Najia's fortune? I myself, with my own two hands, have brought her proposals from four different men!

"The first is a cousin of mine, with a job that pays a decent salary and a house to his name to boot. A comfortable man from a good family. And the second suitor—forgive me for not saying his name—he's a merchant whose clout in the market runs deep. And the third is our neighborhood mukhtar, Saeed Abu-Abdullah—you all know him. As for the fourth, he's like an angel from heaven, not to mention his wealth and properties—the man has money to burn."

"Didn't Najia like any of them?"

"Ehh, what Najia thinks, my dear, is neither here nor there. Every time I go to speak to her brother about a new proposal—after sounding her out first to make sure she's willing—he'll hear me out, and then he'll look down for a while and twirl his mustache. After that, he'll promise me good news, and then I will go home and they will hold a war council, led by that snake, Umm Shawqy. And the decision will come, as expected:

'Najia sends her apologies; she has no eyes for men after the loss of her husband.'

"And I swear, as God is my witness, that if Najia said anything of the sort, then her brother and his wife and their children put her up to it. As if she could've been in love with that obnoxious oaf Masoud. Anyway, may God forgive his transgressions—it's our duty to pray for the dead. I wish you'd seen Najia eighteen years ago, when they married her off to Masoud. She was only seventeen, and he was a fat widower with a body like a sack stuffed with cotton and a saggy, drooping face. But ask me about his pockets… As rich as Croesus, he was, with a thriving business, and no end to his towering buildings and stores. The poor girl lived with that old goat for eight years with no children to show for it, and then he died from high blood pressure. He was so besotted with the tender Najia that he put everything he owned in her name, and his relatives got nothing.

"And oh, the tears Abu Shawqy and his wife shed, my dear! I swear on your life, if their own son had died, they wouldn't have poured out as many tears as they did over Masoud. They had all the town's sheikhs reading Qur'an for his soul; the sound of it filled the air. And his funeral—they kept it going for forty days and nights! And Najia, like an idiot, would wail every time Umm Shawqy wailed, and every time Abu Shawqy wrung his hands. He'd say, 'There's no power or strength save in God,' and 'I seek refuge in God,' and the tassel on his tarboush would shake as he reeled off the dead man's virtues and wept as if Masoud's death meant more to him than all his departed loved ones combined.

"After the funeral ended, and everyone had paid their respects, Abu Shawqy went up to his sister and swore that Masoud's door would never be closed. No, his house would stay open just as if he was alive and more. And his sister would remain the mistress of her own home, where she belonged.

"But of course Najia, being a woman, needed protection. And she was young and beautiful, and also rich, meaning gold-diggers would be after her money. It made no sense for her to live alone in a huge house where her grief would only grow to fill it and loneliness would strike by midday. And so Abu Shawqy, and Umm Shawqy, and Shawqy himself, along with his brothers and sisters, must come to cure their aunt's sadness, and to keep her company so she wouldn't die of misery over losing Masoud.

"And what a sweet deal it was for them! They sold their furniture, rented out their house, and descended on the aunt as cherished guests. Some guests they were! Najia soon became the guest, and Umm Shawqy the one in charge, giving orders left and right, not a command of hers refused nor a wish disobeyed—all she had to do was humor Najia a bit. Well, Umm Shawqy's happy enough now, lording it over the neighborhood women with her nose stuck up in the sky.

"And Abu Shawqy took over his sister's finances: he bought things and sold things, he moved things around, he changed and exchanged things, and he took what he took, all the while praying for Masoud's soul every time he got up or sat down. He filled the walls with pictures of Masoud and hired Qur'an reciters to read verses of the Holy Book every Friday at his grave. He even celebrated the anniversary of Masoud's death twice a year!

"Ehh, that's how you fool people who should know better! They did all this to fill Najia's head with the man's memory so she wouldn't think of marrying again, like a flighty woman might. And Umm Shawqy kept stirring the pot until she set Najia against me. She went and lied to Najia—it was out-and-out slander!—saying that Umm Youssef goes around telling the neighbors, 'If it wasn't for Najia's money, no suitor would darken her door!' Now, just between us, dear neighbor, that is actually true. It's hard enough, these days, to find a match for girls getting married for the first time, let alone widows!

"Oh well, it's none of my business. Wallah, if I wasn't fond of Najia, and didn't feel bad for how she's being swallowed whole by her brother and his family, I wouldn't have bothered. She must be mad to let Abu Shawqy and his family use her money as if it were their own: the best colleges for his sons, the best husbands for his daughters! But what's it to me, anyway?"

Umm Youssef stood up and wrapped herself in her abaya, saying, "I've run out of stories to entertain you with, but just give me until Abu Shawqy's daughter gets married." Then she broke into a shrill laugh and rushed off to rescue a dish she'd left on the stove.

We didn't see Umm Youssef for days after that. Like everyone in the neighborhood, she was kept away from us by that wedding of Souad—

Najia's niece. The women who had been invited were busy preparing for the event with new clothes and all manner of primping and preening. As for Umm Youssef, well, Umm Shawqy hadn't invited her. She was too careful to allow the wedding to be used as an excuse for mending broken bridges. Still, the occasion had spurred her—meaning Umm Youssef—into a flurry of activity. A piece of news here, a story there: she was gathering ammunition that would keep her in gossip for more than a month!

She passed by before the wedding and said, "Good news, my dear! Najia has bought a colorful dress, new shoes, and makeup for the wedding. And she's put away her black clothes. It's a good start—rain begins with a single drop!" Her familiar laugh rang out, then she slipped away, just as she had come, in a hurry. Another time, she looked in on us and made a show of flipping her hair, "I saw Najia yesterday, on her way back from the hairdresser's, flashing a toothy grin. When she walked past our door, she turned and greeted me, as friendly as can be, and asked about my health and the children's. I'll show you, Umm Shawqy, just you wait. All I need is a month, one more month."

After that, we heard from women in the neighborhood that the ice had thawed between Najia and Umm Youssef, and that Najia—taking advantage of her sister-in-law's preoccupation with the wedding and all its trappings—had begun to visit Umm Youssef every few days. And we heard about, and saw, Najia in a style of clothing very different from the crow-like black that we'd been used to seeing her wear. Perhaps being caught up in all this lengthened the gaps between Umm Youssef's visits. But one evening she showed up, in a rush as usual. And as soon as my mother subtly probed for news of Najia, Umm Youssef said, "Just between us, dear neighbor, Souad's wedding has brought out a whole new Najia: dresses in greens and reds, perfumed hair, scarlet nails, high-heeled shoes. It's not Masoud's grave she's focused on now. Subhanallah, what a change! The sight of a bride getting ready for her wedding has stirred up Najia's passions and emotions, and it's threatening all of Umm Shawqy's well-laid plans.

"Yesterday, I told Najia that my only wish in this world is to see her a bride, and that one word from her was all it would take to bring her an entire troop of suitors, so she could choose someone who deserved her. The words were barely out of my mouth when she said, 'Wallah, you're a good friend, Umm Youssef. And I can tell that you only want what's best for me, so do whatever you see fit.'"

A sly smile spread over Umm Youssef's face as she said, "Just between us, dear neighbor, it's nature's way, and Najia's only human. Wallah, I won't rest until I see her married—and Umm Shawqy's nose rubbed in the dust."

BUT UNTIL THEN

"Don't get up, Souad. Stay where you are—I'll bring you breakfast in bed."

Souad had been about to push back the bedcovers when her aunt reached out to stop her. "No, don't get up! Stay in bed. I heard you coughing yesterday, and I'm worried you might catch a cold."

Souad's cough wasn't serious, and it certainly didn't call for her aunts to spoil her with breakfast in bed. But she knew what was behind it, so she stretched out lazily in the bed, a canny smile playing on her lips as she pondered this sudden change in the atmosphere.

Before, she had to wake up at dawn, and walk—on her own two feet—to the kitchen to make coffee and breakfast for herself and her two aunts. And if she'd happened to sleep in for a few minutes, then her older aunt's voice would ring out:

"Isn't the pasha's daughter up yet? Masha' Allah! Does she think she can sleep till noon? And then who's supposed to sweep the balcony and water the plants? Me?

Quickly, before a curse could jump to her aunt's lips, Souad would scramble out of bed and set about attending to the household business.

She had Fahmy—the neighbors' son—to thank for this change of heart, and even more thanks were due to the neighbors' maid, who had come round the day before on an errand for her mistress, and had been met with hospitality that was quite out of character for Souad's aunts. In a bout of calculated generosity, the maid was allowed a cup of coffee and a piece of candied bitter orange. After that, details about her employers rolled freely off her tongue. There was Fahmy, the family's eldest son, a kind and well-mannered boy who had just earned "the big certificate," having graduated from university that year. Then there was Laila, his spoiled younger sister: all she cared about was reading French novels, playing the piano, and going to the movies with her friends. As for their mother, Umm Fahmy, she was a lady of leisure, a cosseted woman with a maid, driver, and cook, who had her breakfast brought to her in bed.

The maid's words were still buzzing in the aunts' ears when she left, and they exchanged a look of secret understanding.

So this morning, Souad's food was carried to her in bed! But we must all be wondering about the secret behind this sudden and unaccustomed pampering of the orphan girl, who had been raised by two aging aunts. Well, it happened that, for a number of reasons, the aunts thought that Fahmy—the son of the well-known doctor whose family had recently moved in next door—had his eye on Souad.

Shafiqa, the older aunt, had been out on the balcony one day when she saw her niece exchanging smiles with a young man on the neighboring balcony. She had been about to unleash a screech that would freeze the smile on the girl's lips when she remembered that the balcony the boy was standing on belonged to the rich, distinguished doctor with the chauffeur-driven car, the one who lived in the villa that passersby gawped at with great envy. Her mouth took on a shape that dithered between a smile and a scowl, echoing her uncertainty. Should she make it an outright smile? Or exchange it for a conventional scowl that would show the pair of them that the aunt didn't like, or condone, such forward behavior?

She caught them again in the act of smiling. This called for an urgent interrogation, and the aunts had taken turns asking questions.

"How did you meet the boy?"

"He sees me on the balcony sometimes, and we've crossed paths a couple of times on the street."

"Did you speak to each other?"

The girl coughed, trying to avoid having to answer, but a stern glare from the older aunt loosened her tongue.

"Yes," she said.

"Well, what did he say?"

"He asked how my aunts were doing."

The aunts gave each other a look, and spoke in one voice, "Did he really say that? Such a well-bred young man... well-bred indeed. And what else?"

"Once he saw me on the tram and paid for my ticket."

Shafiqa frowned and feigned a stern expression. "All right," she said, "go and get on with your chores."

As soon as Shafiqa and Anisa were alone, they set aside the embroidery they had been working on.

"Do you think...?" the younger one asked her sister.

"Yes, I do think. And why not? It's all down to her and how clever she can be. He's not too grand to fall in love with Souad and marry her, is he? Is there any girl in the neighborhood prettier than Souad? She may be poor compared to him, but there's no shame in being poor—I've heard Umm

Fahmy herself was once a nurse at her husband's clinic. And our girl is polite and gracious, she leads a modest life at home, and was educated by nuns to boot. There's never been a shameful word said about a woman from the house of Abu Fares! All this needs from us is a bit of friendliness, a little tact, and some maneuvering.

Tomorrow, without delay, you and I will go visit the boy's mother."

"But—"

"But what? Do you mean to say we don't know her? So what? Let's get to know her. How do you think people get to know each other, anyway, if they've met in the street or at the market? Don't worry, it's not a sin in anyone's book to pursue a good, proper match. Do you want people to say the Abu Fares girls all end their days as spinsters? Or if they do marry, it's late in life, when they're dried-up old women? No, not another word from you, I know what you're going to say. You're a spinster by choice? No my dear, no. Not a single man has come knocking at your door—apart from Isaac the sausage seller who was deaf and had one foot in the grave. You just stay quiet, stay quiet, Anisa. I know better than you do about these things. Fabric and threads are all you know of the world. Tomorrow—as I said—we'll visit Umm Fahmy and encourage her and her daughter to visit us."

Anisa stayed quiet. In all her fifty years, she'd never had the pleasure of having a wish of hers carried out—not while Shafiqa was around. They had grown up together and learned their craft together. Their embroidery was well-known: under their skilled fingers, fabric was stretched out on embroidery frames and deftly transformed into linens to adorn the homes of new brides.

Shafiqa was the one who met with the customers. She made the arrangements and accepted the payments. She was careful with what she spent of their money—it pained her to part with every piaster. And the piasters, all those saved-up piasters, would come in handy on a rainy day. After all, the sisters' future was far from assured, once their eyesight lost its sharpness and their only source of income was cut off. Anisa had briefly escaped from under her sister's thumb when Shafiqa got married, but it had been a short union that passed as quickly as a summer night. The elderly husband died without leaving any children, and Shafiqa went back to her old ways at home, back to the embroidery frames and back to ordering Anisa around.

The elder sister got her way, and they visited Umm Fahmy. For a reason known only to Shafiqa, they didn't take Souad along, and they came home an hour later, the world having shrunk in their eyes, its affairs now confined to Fahmy's family: his mother, his father, his sister, their luxurious home and its sumptuous furniture. They didn't run out of things to say for an entire evening that lasted until well after midnight—they were so absorbed in their conversation that they forgot it cost money to keep the lights on.

Overhearing them, Souad's feminine intuition told her that her aunt was plotting something, and that she'd given serious weight to the innocent smiles and casual greetings between her and the boy. But she said nothing, waiting to see how things would develop, or perhaps giving in to her aunts' pampering. She'd been let off from most of her household duties; her aunts had realized that scrubbing the floor would spoil the softness of her hands, and that it was imprudent to have an elegant woman peel onions. As for sweeping the balcony, and especially the balcony across from the neighbors' house, it was unbefitting of someone whose sights—or whose aunts' sights—were set on a high-society man like Fahmy.

"Souad, why don't you invite the boy over for a cup of coffee?"

The girl was embarrassed. How could she do that? Or rather, how could she manufacture the right moment to ask? She didn't answer, and her cheeks flushed red.

"Oh dear, you're feeling shy," her aunt said kindly. "Never mind, I'll invite him myself…"

An opportunity soon presented itself: She was walking down the street with Souad when he happened to walk past, offering a quiet greeting on his way. But Shafiqa thought it her absolute duty not to pass by without exchanging a few pleasantries, and she slowed him down by inquiring about his mother, his father, and the health of the nice young lady—his sister. She chatted on and asked how he was spending his vacation. "We're neighbors," she said, "and we'd be delighted if you stopped by for a visit. You're such a nice young man, and we're good friends with your mother."

He thanked her politely and, by the time she'd finished talking, they'd reached home. She insisted he come in, so he did, after casting a glance at his house to see if anyone was looking. The coffee, candies, and American cigarettes—bought in a rush by Anisa from the nearest shop—were soon ready, and the boy stayed for an hour. When he left, the aunts walked him to the bottom of the stairs and showered him with invitations to "come again."

As for Souad, she sat wondering anxiously what the boy had made of her aunts. Her thoughts were interrupted by Shafiqa's voice; she had returned to the room and was gently chastising her for not making enough of an effort to get along with Fahmy: Souad had been so quiet he might think his visit had been unwelcome, or that she didn't know how to string two words together. Shafiqa offered Souad some advice, then turned to Anisa and whispered, "Our son-in-law is a very nice boy, don't you think?"

Chance played a role in the aunts' dreams when Fahmy's sister stopped by to order some embroidery for a dress. They welcomed her with cheerful smiles and offered to teach her the craft so she could embroider the dress herself.

Laila welcomed the suggestion. This would be a new experience, a refreshing change from the leisurely pursuits of her comfortable life. With needle and fabric in hand, she began to visit them every day. In time, she and Souad grew close, with much encouragement from the aunts. And Laila invited her new friend to her birthday party. Souad didn't go empty-handed, of course. Shafiqa had given her a cheerful, spring-colored curtain to take as a gift. And Souad was made even happier by the fruits of her aunts' prudence: Shafiqa had opened her purse strings wide to buy her a new dress and a pair of shoes. She was to look as elegant as the best of the women invited, a delicate flower who would captivate everyone who saw her. Fahmy would be there, and he'd see her, and they'd talk, and... and who knows!

Souad went to the party feeling a little shy, as she had never met young people like these before. Laila caught sight of her and hurried over to say hello, and she soon found herself caught up in the spirit of the party. Dance music started to play, and the young partygoers grew louder, their clamoring voices blowing away the stuffy atmosphere that reigns over the beginnings of parties, when people are interested only in getting the measure of everyone who comes in, and each new arrival is met with gazes of admiration, ridicule, or approval.

Meanwhile, Shafiqa and Anisa were looking out from their balcony, watching the partygoers—in other words, the female partygoers—and wondering who the unfamiliar faces might be. The large number of young women at the party made Shafiqa uncomfortable. "Laila has... so many girlfriends," she said.

Anisa caught her sister's meaning, and said, "Don't worry, not a one of them is prettier than our Souad."

They stayed where they were on the balcony, eaten up with anxiety, until Souad came home to share news of the party, and to answer the questions that came at her like pelting rain.

Did you say hello to Umm Fahmy? Did you dance with Fahmy? What did Laila say about your dress? Who was that blonde in the green dress? You didn't get to meet her? We need to ask around—she's a snob, isn't she? One look at her was enough to tell us that! Oh—Laila told you to always put your hair up like that? See? We told you so! We know your sister-in-law's taste better than you do—you must keep that hairstyle.

Shafiqa couldn't rest until she found out who the stuck-up blonde in the green dress had been. After a while, she learned that the girl's mother was a frequent visitor at the doctor's house. This annoyed Shafiqa. What right did that woman have to drag her daughter there every other day? She knew, better than anyone, all about scheming women like that one, women whose only concern was to hunt for husbands for their daughters. But this... this was going too far; she shouldn't be allowed to get away with it! Fahmy was definitely fond of Souad. All the signs pointed to it: he smiled at her from the balcony, he spoke to her in the street, and once he gave her a book. And his sister liked her so much that she invited her to their family parties. Even the maid swore that Laila often spoke well of Souad to her mother.

The family's intentions were as clear as day! So why were this woman and her daughter trying to stand in their way? No, Shafiqa would give it a little time, but if this woman didn't stay away, she would go to the woman's house herself and warn her to stop her devious ways. Yes! And she'd make sure to tell her about Fahmy's feelings for Souad.

The cheek of those women!

Anxiety kept eating away at the aunts—especially Shafiqa. The boy still hadn't popped the question. So when would he? He must be planning to do it soon. Perhaps he was busy thinking about his future. He couldn't very well propose to a girl from a good family before he'd settled on something, could he?

They knew someone would inevitably make a move, and their worst fear was that a ploy from the other girl's mother would turn the boy's head, leaving Souad with nothing but heartache. And so Shafiqa and Anisa carried on, with Souad at the top of their worries. In the aunts' minds, the road to their precious son-in-law was strewn with hope. But the girl remained neutral—what lay between her and the boy hadn't been enough to convince her to share her aunts' ambitions. She lay back peacefully in her pampered cocoon, waiting expectantly for the end of the story.

And one day, the end came.

The aunts woke to the sound of the neighbors bidding farewell to their son. He was going away to study in America.

And Souad woke from a night of dreams about Fahmy—she built castles in the sky more boldly while dreaming than when awake. She woke to the familiar sound of Shafiqa shouting, "Isn't the pasha's daughter up yet? Does she think she can sleep till noon? And then who's supposed to sweep the balcony and water the plants? Me?"

PINK CURTAINS

Abu Khalil was a venerable old spice merchant whose store, which stood at the corner of the neighborhood, filled the air with rich aromas of cinnamon, cloves, cardamom, and henna. He was a connoisseur of women, but only within the realm of the halal, and he never kept more than two or three wives at a time.

As for the number of women who happened to have once upon a time been a part of his harem, there were more than ten of them. But the only one Abu Khalil had not divorced and sent on her way was his first wife.

They say he kept her in recognition of her good character, and for the sake of Mahmoud, their son, who was his beloved favorite. There came a time when he had no wives but her, and we all thought he had given up his hobby and preferred now to live out a quiet old age, unmarred by the fighting and scheming amongst his women.

All, that is, except my mother. She refused to believe that the man had repented and turned over a new leaf. She swore that, at the mere glimpse of a woman walking through the alley, he would stick his tarboushed head out through the store's door and inspect her from head to toe, then scurry to comb his short, henna-dyed beard with stiff fingers.

We knew Abu Khalil from his store, and he was our neighbor, too, the owner of an old house that stood next door to ours. We could look into his house through a small window in the middle of the ancient kitchen wall. He had once housed one of his women there. She was a seductress; as soon as Abu Khalil devoted a night to her, she would pin a huge flower to her head, fixing it to the edge of the brilliant scarf tied around her hair, and slathering her face with assorted dyes. Before long, the rhythmic beats of a tabla would rise, and his first wife, Umm Mahmoud, would hear of it. But she would just laugh, saying, "Only The Everlasting is everlasting. He'll divorce her soon enough."

And "soon enough" would take two or three months, or a year at the outside, but it never went past a year. The house had wives constantly moving in and out, until a rumor went round the neighborhood that Abu Khalil had decided to reward Umm Mahmoud for her forbearance by devoting himself to her and her six sons and daughters, and to the two boys he'd had by other wives. One of them was still in his mother's custody, but the other had joined his father's household, where he ate and slept under Umm Mahmoud's kind care and waited with his siblings for the time when he would get his share of his father's inheritance.

But my mother still refused to believe this whole repentance business. If it had been genuine, she said, he would have rented out the two rooms, instead of leaving them unoccupied "for emergencies." The man had an appetite for life's pleasures, and he still had an eye for women.

And she was right. We were sitting with some of the neighborhood women on the bench outside our house when we saw the window in the room facing our kitchen open up, and a woman dusted off the rickety frame. My mother jumped to her feet and nudged our neighbor, saying, "Told you so, didn't I? Abu Khalil has a new wife."

We stood up and stared nosily at the face looking out of the window. It was the dried-up face of an old woman whose head was covered with a white scarf. We thought it unlikely that she was the bride, seeing as Abu Khalil's taste in wives ran to heavy hips and eyes with perfectly arched eyebrows. Large bosoms were also a must, and he would insist on painting the women's hands with henna from his shop.

The news spread through the neighborhood, and, from each window, a woman hung out her head and winked at her neighbor. All eyes remained fixed on Abu Khalil's house until he arrived in the evening, leaning on a stick and dressed up in what the neighborhood women called his "wedding-night suit": a pair of sirwal-style pants which covered his short legs, and a waistcoat with a gold watch chain hanging from its pocket. He reeked of rose attar and his beard shone with henna, confirming our suspicions beyond a doubt. That night we held more than one gathering and entertained ourselves by digging up Abu Khalil's past and picking over the story of his life with many wives.

We waited breathlessly for morning to come so we could check out the bride to see if she was fair or dark, thin or fat, a seductress like the one he'd just divorced, or a naïve woman who had been pushed by circumstances into marriage.

We didn't rest until the day after his wedding, when the curtain was drawn and a plump, white face looked out through eyes that kohl had failed to widen. The window soon opened, and a woman leaned her head out into the street. She looked young, barely twenty years old, which made my mother grind her teeth and say, "God curse him! What's to be done with a man who has no shame? The older he gets, the more foolish he grows!"

And when the woman saw us gaping at her, she smiled a rather stupid smile, chomped a few times on a piece of gum in her mouth, and disappeared behind the ancient curtain. We didn't see her again until three days later when Abu Khalil left to see to his affairs, his short legs plodding steadily toward his store, his potbelly leading the way.

As soon as the neighborhood women felt the coast was clear, they decided to visit the bride. They would hurry over to her house to be treated to coffee and cigarettes. And each of them would volunteer to be a friend and a sister to her, so they'd find out the circumstances that bound this plump, soft-skinned creature to the dried-up old man, and bring home a tale to feed their banter for days.

They came back, having unanimously decided that the girl must be from a miserably poor family. Otherwise she never would have been satisfied with marrying Abu Khalil, living like a pauper and letting him get away with not providing what husbands usually did for a marriage. Indeed, there was nothing in their room except a bed that had belonged to four or five wives before her, a battered old wardrobe, and some chairs with wobbly legs. And amongst all her clothes, there was not a single outfit befitting a radiant bride.

Yes, she must come from poverty. Why else would her mother be living with them?

One of the women said, "This must be her old mother's doing. She married her to him in the hopes that he'd die and she'd inherit."

Another said, "Our friend was thinking only of her stomach when she agreed to marry him. Don't you see her jaws constantly working when she looks out the window?"

And, pulling her black milaya around her as she prepared to leave, a third woman said, "Don't you worry about her. You mark my words, if anything will be the end of Abu Khalil, it'll be this greedy cow."

At this, squeals of laughter broke out in the room.

I don't know why I remembered the woman's prediction three months later, when there was an insistent knocking at our door, and we heard Umm Fahima—Fahima being the name of Abu Khalil's young wife—asking my mother where the nearest doctor was, because Abu Khalil had suffered a chest attack caused by his high blood pressure. My mother directed her to the neighborhood doctor, and she immediately rushed to fetch him. Umm Fahima, after moving in next door, had begun stopping by to see us every now and then. She would hunker down near the door and reach between her breasts to pull out a tin box that she'd filled with fine-cut tobacco. Then she'd roll herself a cigarette, which emerged saggily from between her fingers, almost falling apart, and she'd light it, gulping down the smoke with relish.

We would ask her why she didn't bring Fahima with her, and she'd say, "You must excuse her. Her husband is the jealous type and doesn't allow her to mix with any of the neighborhood women, so that nobody spoils her relationship with him. She stays in the house when he's there, and when he's gone, too, in case he sends his shop assistant to check on her and she's not there when he comes." When we grew more familiar with each other, my mother felt she had the right to ask Umm Fahima why she had married her daughter to that oft-marrying old goat. "Marriage gives a girl protection," she said. "I was afraid she'd go naked and hungry, and there are so many shady bastards out there. He seemed to be rich; I mean, he bought her a couple of bangles, a pair of earrings, three dresses, and a dozen bars of perfumed soap, so I married her to him. If he lives, she can live off his wealth, and if he dies, she can marry someone else. Isn't she better off like this, than if she'd married a young man who beat her every night, like her father used to do with me?"

My mother's curiosity didn't stop there, so she asked whether her daughter had hopes of an inheritance. The woman's face fell a little, and she said, "Wallah my dear neighbor, I can't hide the fact that my daughter is a fool. She couldn't get him to promise her anything, and, if he were to die, Umm Mahmoud would never let her see a penny of his fortune—we don't even know if it's big or small. And the worst thing is that she hasn't fallen pregnant. Nothing worked to make it happen, not medicine and not the talisman Sheikh Barakat prescribed for her. This daughter of mine is like her mother: short on luck." And we saw a cloud of sorrow descend on the woman's face.

This was before she came knocking on our door to ask about a doctor. Then the man fell ill, and his condition became critical. Umm Mahmoud started sending one of her sons to the house every half hour, to check how Abu Khalil was doing, and Umm Fahima would rush over to our place every half hour to smoke a hand-rolled cigarette. "We plan, fate laughs," she would say. "High blood pressure never crossed our minds. If he dies, Umm Mahmoud will kick us out of the room, she won't let us spend a single night in the house. We've heard it's all in her name, you see; Abu Khalil gave it to her. We were fools to have been so obliging that we didn't even ask for proper furniture. I was planning to get Fahima to press him for it, if he hadn't fallen ill."

I don't know if my mother was serious or joking when she advised the woman to urge Fahima to wait for the right moment, and then ask him to pledge before God that he would fill her room with furniture if God granted him a full recovery, but Umm Fahima liked the suggestion—the creases on her forehead smoothed out, and she said, "Sounds like a sensible plan… He's more attached to life than a twenty-year-old."

She left us in a hurry and, two days later, came back satisfied, saying, "It worked just as you said. He has promised that, if he is cured, he'll buy her two beds and a new wardrobe, and a beast that he'll slaughter at their door for Eid Al-Adha."

And the man recovered, we don't know how. Was it the doctor's expertise? The intercession of saints? Umm Fahima's pledges? One morning, after he left for his store, Umm Fahima rushed over to our house, clutching some money. She told us that Abu Khalil had given her money for a new curtain and promised, for his part, to stop by the market and order the beds and the wardrobe.

The woman left and soon came back with a length of fabric, which she turned over to my mother for her to trim the edges and make a curtain from it. When my mother gave it back to her, the tattered, faded old curtain disappeared and the new one came out, shining as pink and bright as Fahima's cheeks.

And on the day the new furniture was delivered, Abu Khalil came back earlier than usual in the evening; it was clear his beard was freshly dyed. More than one eyelid, belonging to more than one neighbor, fluttered in sly winks.

Two weeks went by, and every morning the curtain would open, and Fahima's rosy face would look out, with the gum going round and round in her mouth. She would ask us how we were, and she would flash us her meaningless smile.

Then one day, we didn't see Fahima, as we usually did in the morning. Instead, we saw her mother as she rushed past our door on her way to summon the doctor from his clinic to examine Abu Khalil.

The woman raced by, and heads sprouted at the windows. The winking started again, tongues began to wag, and a sly neighbor's voice bluntly said, "If Abu Khalil dies this time, good riddance! With a pink curtain and new furniture, Fahima won't stay single for more than three days!"

THE LITTLE THINGS

Had she gone too far?

She didn't know, and she wasn't sure she wanted to find out. All she wanted was to live in this beautiful feeling, to make it last, to take something new and different into her shell with her. Everything in her universe was dwarfed by this feeling, even her parents, her aunt, her teachers.

They could all go to hell!

She'd had enough of her family's preaching. From now on, when she heard it—either in the morning or the evening, or whenever she was going out, even just to stroll down the road—she'd reply with a pitying smile and a philosophical toss of her head, as her ears, her heart, and her soul had rejected what she heard until she could mock her old values.

They didn't understand, and she herself had only just started to figure things out!

Now she wouldn't be hurt when her friends said, "You fool! You have the same mentality as your parents and your spinster aunt!"

It was true. She used to be like them, all three of them, but now she had a new sense of the world. And after today, she'd rely on her own feelings and her own free will to define herself, not on the words of her mother and father and spinster aunt: "Don't be like the others, you're nothing like those frivolous girls, you're this, and you're that…"

Tomorrow, her girlfriends from class were meeting under the scraggy old oak tree, and they'd talk about everything and nothing. Hands would carefully reach into pockets, bringing out the perfumed letters that had captured the girls' eyes and hearts. And, for the first time, she would have something to say, if she chose to speak. She had plenty of stories to tell about him. And even if she stayed quiet—and shyness might well stop her from speaking—it wouldn't be because she had nothing to say, but because she had chosen discretion. In any case, she'd tell herself the story with all the tiny details she knew so well; she relived them every time she threw her head onto the pillow, or huddled, dreaming, in the corner of the bus, or tuned out of a lesson, hearing only the bell that marked its end. His face was always near; she'd conjure it up whenever she let her eyelids fall, and it would come to her, jumbled at first, then settling into its familiar shape, so she could clearly make out the tanned brown forehead, the dark brown eyes, and the smile, which was the best thing about his face.

She wished it was only an hour until she could join her lovestruck friends. She would scream, without shame, "He's THE ONE!"

How large he loomed in her world! But all her friends cared about was finding out his name. Who had turned the smug, stubborn girl she used to be into a silly female, just like them?

What would they say if they knew the stubbornness had been knocked right out of her that first time she saw his brown face on the bus?

They'd laugh at her, of course, but they'd realize she was human, and that, just like them, she had feelings and could fall in love! Didn't they call her "the wooden plank?" She used to scoff at this, waving them off with a flick of her wrist. She'd taken comfort in what her mother and father and aunt always said: that she wasn't like the others, she was cut from a different cloth, came from a purer stock, and was the perfect example of how a girl should be.

What a fool she'd been!

The first time was on the microbus. He had climbed in and, without even a glance at her, sat in the seat next to hers. But she saw his reflection in the driver's mirror and liked the color of his hair and the shape of his bottom lip. He got off before her, and she went off to college and forgot all about him.

The second was at a shop that sold soft drinks. Feeling thirsty one day, she'd gone in with her books to order something and saw he was there. She drank up without looking at him, then tried to pay with a large note. The seller apologized—he didn't have change—so she turned to the boy and asked him to break the bill. Then she paid for her drink, glad he hadn't offered to buy it for her, like some insolent boys would.

The third time was at the library, where she'd gone to read the chapters she'd been assigned from The Unique Necklace, only to find him there, hunched over a book (perhaps, like her, he was a student of literature). She settled down to her reading, but when she lifted her head, she caught him staring at her face. This made her happy, but she didn't smile at him.

The fourth, fifth, and tenth times were also chance meetings at the library. She was done with The Unique Necklace, but she kept going back to read it, hoping every time to see him. Once she'd arrived and reassured herself that he was there, his head bent over a book, she would breathe a sigh of relief, making her way to her place with a little skip in her step.

Still, she never once forgot that she wasn't like the others, and that—as her parents and spinster aunt would say—she was cut from a different cloth. So she would greet him primly, and then turn with restless attention to her book. She read, but struggled to understand and, every now and then, would nervously jerk her head up to steal a glance at the nearby brown face.

Once, she had noticed he was stirring in his chair and closing his book, so she jumped up and rushed to return hers to the librarian, making it to the staircase before him. Then his footsteps echoed behind her, and she could tell he was close. He smiled at her, and they walked down the stairs together, and headed—also together—for the bus. He asked if he could sit with her, and insisted on paying for her ticket. She had started to object, but his smile, which had a hint of teasing, made her stop. And on the way, he found out what her name was, and the name of the college she attended, and she found out his name, and that he wasn't a student like she'd thought.

She liked his name. And she was glad he wasn't just some naive student.

And when they parted, she had felt a bit anxious, worried that she'd been nicer to him than she should have been. And she was afraid that curious eyes might have seen them together. But, deep down, she gave in to the strange feeling that had swept over her.

After that, she often ran into him without having arranged to meet, encounters for which she believed chance alone was responsible. After all, she wasn't flighty and he wasn't reckless, so she ruled out the thought of any scheming.

Once, she was standing in line to buy a ticket at the cinema. She had bought her ticket and turned around to find him waiting his turn behind her. He nodded hello, and she rushed in and sat in her place, feeling a little nervous and confused. Not long after, he came and sat down in the seat beside hers. She had pondered this move. Had he sat there on purpose, or by chance? She had begun to wonder whether these repeated coincidences were too opportune to be pure chance. So why was this person following her? Why was he paying her so much attention? If he was doing it deliberately, then she would resist him, firmly, and she'd keep him in line. Because, of course, she wasn't like the others. She was different from them in both seed and nurture, with principles she had never betrayed. And this sort of thing was forbidden by her upbringing and her father, her mother, and her aunt. And she… she… she had ignored him. She hadn't spared him a single glance. Still, in spite of all that, her heart had sunk when he got up and left the theater, although he soon came back with a bag of candy. He had offered her some, but she refused. Without a word, he smiled a smile that lit up his brown features, and cruelly ate it all himself.

The film started, and images crowded onto the screen, but she watched with unseeing eyes, distracted by the one sitting next to her. Why had he come? And what did he want from her? Why didn't he try to start a conversation? Had it been rude to refuse his candy? How silly she'd been! What would it have mattered if she'd eaten a little, when she'd already let him pay for a bus ticket? Surely by now they knew each other well enough. Or didn't she think their sessions in the serious atmosphere of the library, surrounded by the smell of books, meant she could feel at ease in the company of this nice, polite young man?

What was this feeling that stirred inside her every time he was near? Anxiety? Confusion? Elation? Was it happiness or anger? Or was it all of those combined?

Even though it was dark, she had sensed his eyes staring at her face, making her heart pound hard in her chest, and leaving her so unsettled that all she could make out on the screen were shadows. He had some nerve! If he went any further, she would scream at him and… She felt his hand inching closer to hers, his fingers reaching longingly for hers, and she didn't pull them away—her fingers felt like they were glued to the armrest. He smoothed his palm over the back of her hand, closing his fist around it, holding it tight. And they stayed like that until the lights came on. She felt annoyed that the ending had come so soon, and then was ashamed of herself, despising her weakness. She left without looking at his face.

And that night, she couldn't settle her restless head on her pillow… Had she fallen in love?

She had never been in love before, so how could she know if these unsettling feelings were love? If she asked one of her experienced girlfriends, they would diagnose her case like an expert, dwelling gleefully on the details. But no, she wasn't known for being weak, and she didn't want people to think that she was like the others, that she had… indiscretions. If romance novels were true, then this was love, with all its sweetness and its anxiety. It tormented her night and day, taking over her thoughts and making her forget everyone around her, except when their faces were right in front of her. She'd be called to a meal, but she'd hardly eat a thing, and she'd sit alone with a book, but see only his face. Indeed, she lost all interest in the things she used to enjoy. So then, she realized, she was just like those heroines—the ones in books and movies—even though her hero was different from the ones whose stories we saw on-screen: their bodies were fitter and their features finer than her young man's. Before— because her life had been divided in two parts, "before" she'd met him and "after"—so before, if she sat down and let her imagination run free, as every girl does, to picture the man of her dreams, she would have wished he had wider eyes, and a finer nose. And she would have chosen a cleft chin for him, and a face that wasn't so dark.

But could she really consider him to be hers—had he said so himself?

Did he add all these little things up in the same way she did? If she looked at it objectively, nothing they had done seemed dangerous. What was wrong with a boy talking to her, or paying for her bus ticket just once? A lot of other boys would have been happy to do the same if she'd let them. And what did it matter if his hand had touched hers in a moment of weakness? No, it didn't mean anything—she was just deluding herself. She had given these little things too much significance, until they had grown too big for her little heart to bear, and she'd named this giant she'd created "love."

Secretly, she decided not to make room for him in her heart or her soul; she would turn away from him like a virtuous young woman should—otherwise, what was the difference between her and any of those silly girls?

She had been relieved by this decision, but it crumbled as soon as she saw him a few days later in the street. Her emotions ran riot inside her when he came up with the nicest smile, saying hello and inviting her warmly for a cup of tea. Flustered, she wasn't sure what to say, but she found herself, under the force of his will, sitting in a lovely, quiet café with a cup of tea in front of her, which she drank without tasting. And while they sat there, she no doubt only opened her mouth to say silly things that would break the silence and turn the boy's eyes away from hers.

They finished their tea and got up to go, not to the busy street that led to the world of people, but to another one that twisted and turned until it took them to an open stretch of land. Nothing stirred or made a sound except the swish of their footsteps moving through the grass as they walked, his hand in hers, emotions raging in her heart. She wanted him to take her back to the crowds, but she didn't ask him to do it. And, as if he had read her mind and sensed the struggle in her heart, he pulled her to him and said, "Don't be afraid. I love you."

She didn't say anything—she couldn't say anything—because his lips were on hers, gentle and warm.

Had she gone too far?

She didn't know, and she didn't want to know. All she could think, or feel, or understand was this new sense of life, born this hour inside her.

A SILKEN DREAM

Souad was oblivious to the crowded street. She hardly noticed the shoppers drifting back from their day's rounds, or the cars that stood in an endless row, each one creeping forward just as far as the brief distance between one and the next allowed, or the neon lights dancing in harmony on the roofs and the fronts of the buildings, either pleasing the eye or annoying it.

She pressed her forehead to the glass, her eyes growing rounder as she gawped at the dress in the window, which she had coveted—and still coveted—ever since it was draped on the mannequin's body to tantalize every passing daughter of Eve.

She sighed for the twentieth time, persuaded against the dress by the two hundred lira the store was asking for it. That price tag shattered the dreams of girls like her.

Where would she get two hundred lira? It was two full months' salary, and that same salary was meant for food and rent and clothing and the tram which, every morning and every evening, carried her away from her home in Furn al-Shubbak and back again. And she had her mother and little brother to think about, since she, being the strongest, was the only "man of the family."

Two hundred lira! Was there any woman so gripped by mad desire that she would throw away two hundred lira on a single dress?

If there was such a madwoman, or even more than one, Souad wouldn't have blamed them; the dress was sexy and elegant, and women's wills were weak when faced with the charms of silk.

No, the two hundred lira wasn't too much for it—not for other women, at least—not for one of those women who extended their plump, idle white hands to her, so she could busy herself with their nails, coating them with red polish. The light glinting off the diamond rings on those idle white hands almost stole the light from her eyes.

No, it wasn't too much for them—nor for her with this longing, this desire that gnawed at her: that the dress be hers and no one else's. Her desire for it stemmed from a need that she felt more strongly now than ever before. Would it be the end of the world if she were to have the dress? Oh, how she longed to hold something expensive in her hands, something that didn't come from the Uqiyya Market, where fabric was sold by weight—something that spoke of the blessings of luxury and privilege. Was it too much for her to look, just once, like one of the clients at the shop where she worked? Souad could have sworn she'd never seen one of them in the same dress twice, or wearing shoes with dust from the street on their soles. They were always perfectly coiffed, with manicured nails for which they paid good money, so that they always shone crimson. Nothing bothered a woman like that except if her plans for the evening were lukewarm, or if she was tired after she'd been out late the night before. Her clients spoke to her of these things as she sat plying their nails with her small scissors, or they would talk amongst themselves while waiting for their turn, and she would listen in on their casual chatter, unable to make a single comment. She would sometimes give a knowing laugh, when a new client sat in front of her and asked her to take twice as much care. She knew that, behind that "twice as much," there were trysts and rendezvous galore…

Sometimes she felt jealous when she glimpsed a strange yearning in their beautiful eyes, a restless happiness and a zest for life that she'd never felt, except when she'd met Mansour—and when she had begun to crave that dress. His name floated through her mind, and she passed it through her lips in a whisper. It made her forget the dress and the pot-bellied store owner; instead, Mansour appeared in her thoughts, just as he'd been when she met him at her friend's engagement party. Elegant in his dark blue suit, he had stood out among the young men engrossed in the party, acting the perfect gentleman as he gathered up the bridal dragées that had scattered from her hand when a passerby bumped into her.

She had never seen him before, so she assumed he was a relative or friend of the groom's. And she thought him very charming when he drew close to her and, choosing a moment when the other guests weren't paying attention, said, "It seems the groom missed out by not meeting the bride's friends first!"

He asked her to meet him somewhere the next day.

It was the first time she'd heard such talk, and it embarrassed her, but she couldn't bring herself to be unkind to someone with a smile like his.

So she met him the next day, and they stood chatting for a while, far from curious ears. All she could hear were his whispers, and almost all she saw of his face was his beautiful, gentle smile. She was wrenched away from him by the looming end of her lunch break, as it was time to go back to work.

What had he said to her? She didn't bother trying to recall every detail, but she did remember how keen he'd been to know personal things about her, things she never would have spoken of, if it hadn't been for his persistent, reassuring smile.

Days went by, and her life had a new savor. Work was no longer a chore, since she could look forward to seeing his face when she left in the evening, and she was no longer annoyed by the limp hands and feet lazily extended to her, waiting for their polish.

And yesterday, what a delightful moment it had been—more full of possibility than any other moment in her life—when he invited her to go to a party with him.

A party? Distracted by the happiness and excitement that had washed over her, she had forgotten to ask him where the party was, or to extract more details that could have helped her come up with an excuse to give her mother, so she could explain why she was going out at night looking so elegant, so delicate and pampered…

Elegant? At the thought of that word, she nearly choked, and her anxiety began to rise. How could she be elegant in a dress that she'd worn at least a hundred times, season after season after season? Wouldn't Mansour outshine her in the dark blue suit he'd been wearing the first time they met? She couldn't understand how a printing-press operator like Mansour could own such a stylish outfit. He looked so distinguished in it, like one of those office men. Knowing, as she did, the type of party it would be, wasn't it possible that—in that ancient dress of hers—she would fail the test of facing Mansour's mother and some of his sisters, or maybe all of them? The "mother and sisters" test was never easy, and she had big hopes riding on it.

She wished the dress in the window could be hers.

What would it hurt the store owner if he sold it to her, and collected the price—down to the very last piaster—in installments?

Why not try her luck? Her eyes moved to the man's face, then tracked away from it, following the movement of his hand as he brushed off an insect. But her feet refused to budge. Two hundred lira was two months' salary. Her longing for it was matched only by how far it was out of her reach.

Salesmen were so nasty; they had hearts of stone! But, she wondered, if one of those elegant women with idle hands came into the store, wouldn't the man have agreed to give her a discount, and wouldn't he have bowed in respect while he recorded what she owed in the debts ledger?

Souad let out the sigh of someone whose dreams were beyond her reach, and thought of how she would reflect badly on Mansour if she failed to make sure her appearance was suitably lavish.

Wouldn't Mansour be delighted if he caught sight of her in the dress and feasted his eyes on those flowers, the ones that spread over it like a spring festival?

Two hundred lira! And how would she pay the grocer, the landlord, and the tram conductor what she owed them?

How miserable the dreams of the penniless!

Frustrated, she turned to leave and came face to face with his smile. She felt nervous, as she did every time she met him, and she was even more nervous because he had caught her in such a covetous state.

She could sense the reproach in his eyes, in his smile, and in his words as he patted her shoulder, saying "Good grief, you're not thinking of buying it? Slow down, girl, or else find yourself someone whose claim to elegance comes from more than just second-hand American suits!"

Little by little, her face relaxed, and contentment made its way back to her features. It seemed to her that she had never seen Mansour more manly, or more elegant, than he was at that moment in his cheap khaki shirt.

ON THE ROAD

There goes the bell. I've been waiting for so long! I quickly pull my hand from the tub of water where the empty bottles are piled up, ready to be washed and refilled with beer, then loaded up and taken to the city's bars and nightclubs. There, they're poured straight into mouths whose thirst will never be quenched. They soon come back to me, empty, waiting to be washed.

I look around with restless eyes, searching for a rag. Finding one, I begin to dry my fingers, which are wrinkled from the long soak. I dry them finger by finger, noting where the gold ring is missing from my hand. All my life, I had dreamed of wearing a ring—any ring. One with a shiny red stone, like the ring I used to see in the jewelers' window. I dreamed of wearing it on the ring finger of my right hand. Once, I saved up some money and promised myself the gold ring with the red stone. I didn't know, then, that my father would die, and that I would give the money to my mother and grieve terribly for my father, not allowing myself to think about the ring.

But I have one now: an engagement ring. A simple yellow band that I wear around my finger. He gave it to me when he said, "You shall be my wife." And I was happy—I will be his wife, and I will wear the ring. I longed for him to give me a second ring, along with this yellow band, one with a bit of red on it. But he didn't. He's poor, like me, and he couldn't afford anything more than the engagement ring, a blue silk dress, and a bottle of perfume, which I haven't yet opened.

I reach into my pocket and remove a small leather bag, from which I pluck the ring; I had hidden it away, afraid the soap and water would make it lose its shine. I put the ring on and look around me, realizing that the other women who work here have already slipped away to their nearby homes. Perhaps they are sitting down now, to a warm meal, or lying back in bed. My feet are killing me, but I still need to wait a while in front of the factory, in case he comes by and gives me a lift in the factory truck. I can't bear the thought of walking back to the city on this cold rainy night. Yes, he'll pick me up, along with the crates full of bottles. He can take me home and then make his rounds to deliver the beer. I'll definitely wait. I'm tired, and it's enough that I walked the whole way this morning. I passed so many things: the still-shuttered houses, and people walking to work half-asleep, their eyes full of dreams that hadn't yet faded. I saw women, too, selling eggs and milk, and clouds of smoke forming above the houses' chimneys. And I walked. I walked such a long way to get here—it feels as if the owner built his factory at the ends of the earth. It reminded me of the train I saw as a child, which I always thought was on a journey that went on and on forever, all the way to the ends of the earth. I finally arrived at the same time as the other women who worked at the factory, but I had left home more than an hour before them. My house is far away, in an ancient part of the city. It's where I was born, and where I've lived ever since, and I'm not leaving till I'm married.

Yes, I'm getting married! I have a ring, and a man I love is going to take me home with him. I'll live like a lady—I'll never wash bottles again, nor will I wake up before the roosters, and there will be no more trips between factory and city to make my feet bleed. My man is poor, but he's strong and kind. And I'll look strong beside him, so I won't feel small, the way I do now when one of those elegant, perfumed women walks by. The blue dress he gave me is beautiful, and he's going to buy me another. And he—he's strong and handsome, that's what the girls at the factory said about him. A lot of them were jealous, but some girls wished me well: "You'll be done with all this drudgery," they said the day we got engaged.

One sly girl told me I was such a clever hunter to have snared one of the workers, and barely two months after I started at the factory. I heard it, but I didn't hate her. Perhaps she wished she could find someone who would ease a few of her burdens. She had a right to wish for that: why shouldn't she and I—and all of us—be like those spoiled women who sit gossiping and drinking coffee on their balconies, raising their coffee cups to their lips with plump, ivory-skinned, shiny-ring-adorned hands, and laughing at us whenever we walked past in our ancient clothes?

The road is deserted. The night is muffled by fog. Rain drizzles onto the woolen scarf that I've wrapped around my head. And the truck carrying him and the bottles isn't here yet! Why is he late? Did he leave the factory earlier than usual? Did I miss him leaving in the whirlpool of moving people and machines? I begin to feel afraid. I have a long, long road ahead of me to the ends of the earth, where our ancient house waits, with my silver-haired mother and a pot of soup on the fire. Plus, I'm hungry, and full of longing for my mother and for him. The three of us will sit around the fire and talk about things that look nothing like beer bottles or factory smoke, and dream about things that our lives have never known. Has he passed by without seeing me?

The sound of a car disturbs the night's silence. Perhaps it's him? The glowing eyes appear from afar, and then slowly, slowly come closer. No. It isn't the big truck with its annoying creaks and rattles. It's a rich person's car, nimble and sleek, and he's driving it. But he doesn't stop. Why doesn't he stop? I'm sure he saw me: the car's eyes cut through the dark night, and I stood in its way until I thought it would hit me. And as he drives past, I shout as hard as I can, so he stops. I run to him and he opens the door, but just as I am about to lift my foot, I flinch, sensing the stare of two ugly eyes that bore into me from behind black-rimmed glasses. Who is that? I don't know! Perhaps he is the manager, whom we know only by name. Shifting restlessly in his place, he leans forward a bit, looking me up and down as he asks, "And who the hell is this?" He says nothing more, just waves with his huge cigar for me to move away. And what does the man I love, and who loves me, do? The man who pulled me close and said, "You shall be my wife"? He pushes me away from the door and shuts it in my face—gently or hard, I don't know.

The car drives away, leaving me alone in the storm. A flood of tears boils down my cheeks and a wave of hate surrounds me. Images dance in front of my eyes. Everything seems enormous, unattainable in my weakness, arrogant and haughty, out of reach for people who crawl on their bellies like me. They are all gigantic: houses, people, trees, cars. Even the empty beer bottles are—to me—as tall as giants. And in the middle of this world of towering figures, I see myself with him, with the man who gave me a ring and said, "You shall be my wife." We are midgets, creeping close to the ground. No matter how high we stretch, we can't reach the manager's finger, the finger that, with a mere flick, has pushed me away from the car and left me to the storm.

FROM AFAR

The gown wasn't long. And it wasn't so irksome that he couldn't put up with it for another half an hour. As for the cap, it didn't bother him at all. No, it was quite the opposite: after dreaming about it for so long, he had finally put it on a few days ago, studying himself at length in the mirror before going to the studio. There, he proudly pulled it back on and struck a pompous pose in front of the camera for his graduation photos. His photo would hang on his father's wall, and on the walls of his uncles on both sides of the family, showing every single one of them who he had become. He had considered giving one to her, but couldn't make up his mind about it one way or the other.

And then, as he stood in the long line, waiting for the students from other colleges to get through their ceremonies, he sensed something boring into his back, crumbling his bones and crushing him into someone too slight for the gown he was wearing, too weak to bear the weight of the tasseled cap, too small for the academic degree.

He hadn't caught sight of her yet, but he could feel her eyes behind him. His gut told him that she was there, that she had somehow—he didn't know how—broken through the fences into a world she'd never even dreamed of finding someone to talk to her about, and there she was, pushing through the mass of humanity and choosing a place for herself where she could sit and mock his smallness.

Beads of sweat slid off his forehead, flowing into his eyes, trickling down his back and under his arms, oozing even from between his toes. He was angry, and it was a pointless anger, because there was nothing he could have done to stop her, since she hadn't asked for his help to get in. Even so, her presence rattled him, since it meant the prospect of a scandal about to come to light. Perhaps it was all over and the secret was already out, spilled from the lips of a painted woman who turned this way and that, ignoring the arrogant, disdainful, and disapproving looks that clung to her and saying to everyone, to all the people who had come to cheer at the graduation ceremony, "Look at that tall boy, drowning under the weight of his gown. My tainted money made a doctor of him, and, even so, he begrudged me an invitation. But I came all the same, to shred his pride with my clapping and to remind him that he was made by a woman from the brothels."

A deep loathing came over him as he embraced his anger and wrapped it in a yellow mantle of hate. If only his father had been like the other fathers who had come there to show off their pride, plucking it from the stands, and searching for it in the certificates piled up in front of the dean to be given to their waiting sons and daughters: doctors, engineers, and pharmacists who stood, black-robed, in dignified lines. If his father had been like them, he would have been spared—on this occasion, the one he'd spent his whole life dreaming about—from feeling that he was about to go out into the world with a certificate spattered with the taint of shame.

And when the student on his right gently nudged him, saying, "She's here," his world clouded over, and it seemed that the intense applause for the young woman receiving a degree with honors in engineering wasn't for her—no, it was for the strange story that the other one had volunteered to tell.

His story.

Perhaps it would be a relief when everyone knew his story, since it had already defied the sin-drenched walls and was now available for everyone with ears to hear. He might as well tell it now: he would be good at gathering up the reasons that had made him a victim. Reasons built on the logic that, "I had no choice." Yes, "I had no choice" was the best justification he could give before starting his story.

The first part wasn't even very interesting.

Five years ago, he had arrived in this city a stranger, a young boy from a small village in the Gaza Strip, clutching his high-school certificate. All he had dreamed of was to learn something that would earn him a little distinction and open up a future that was better than being a teacher in one of the Agency's run-down schools.

He knew he had to study hard, never forgetting that, if the Agency hadn't contributed a portion of his fees, the most he could have aspired to was a teaching post, for example, or a job as a clerk at his uncle's law firm.

He sighed. His story was long and difficult; he'd better be brief, as he might soon be called up on stage. In Beirut, he had spent years living like a naïve little mouse, knowing nothing of life's many different spaces, except that he was a student who had no right to take his studies lightly, nor to eat until he felt full, and that, if he ever decided to go to the movies, he would have to skip dinner.

For three years, he had lived like this.

After that, he had learned many things. He learned that the city extended beyond the university's iron gates, and that, despite its small size, it was wider than the blue sea that spread in every direction, as far as the eye could reach.

Yes, he had learned plenty. There was no need to go into the details; all that mattered to anyone was how he'd met her. A colleague of his had introduced them. The more seasoned students liked to have something to hold over their colleagues' heads—it made them look sophisticated, as if they knew more about the world than what could be learned from books.

The first time he met her, he had no idea what people did in such places. She had pitied his confusion so much that she showed him more kindness than strictly dictated by her profession. And before he left, she had returned his money and begged him, by all he held dear, to come back and see her again. Why? He didn't know. Maybe she'd appreciated the exaggerated respect he'd shown her, which he had later laughed about.

And he had gone back, time and again. And they became friends.

In him, she saw someone who could talk to her about a world beyond her small dreams, and in her, he saw something that set her apart from her colleagues, something that made him bring her books and magazines. And perhaps she enjoyed looking educated in front of the others, and behaving in a way that fit with that kind of education.

She was always eager to see him, unlike her other clients, because his visits were times when she felt she could escape from dealing with vulgar whims.

She realized she had grown to love him.

When he visited, she would meet him with her face freshly washed, free from the loud makeup wretched women plastered on themselves. And, even though her vocabulary was weak, she worked hard to read the novels he brought her, showing him how much she cared for his humble gifts.

He was going into too much detail for the short time that was left; the engineers had been given their certificates already, and now the dean of his college was standing up to recite the Hippocratic Oath.

One day, he had been blindsided by a request from his father, who, stricken by asthma, had stopped going to his store. He had asked his son to come back and take over their small business, and then return to university if and when circumstances allowed.

Unbelievable! Had his father lost his mind to ask such a thing, when all he had left until graduation was one short year and part of another? He had refused to go, so his father threatened to cut off the money he sent. Then he made good on his threat, leaving him with nothing but the assistance he received from the Agency.

All he wanted was to do whatever it took to scrape together the tuition money. He always ate at the cafeteria anyway, and it wouldn't hurt him to cut out whatever he could from his routine. He would give up cigarettes and the one or two weekly meals he ate, for a change, at restaurants off-campus.

He didn't know what else to do. In the evening, he had gone to visit her and casually told her what had happened, needing someone to listen and share a few words of sympathy. He had sought nothing more, expected nothing more, and by rights he should have refused if she had offered him anything. What an awful thought it was, for a prostitute to be paying his bills! But she had offered her help, and offered it persistently, begging and imploring him to take it. Was she driven by concern for his future, or fear of losing her educated friend? Perhaps she felt that, by doing this, she would gain society's respect? He didn't know. And he was tired of trying to find an explanation for it, but he was sure her offer had been genuine. He refused. She persisted. He refused. She insisted he should consider it a debt, and that she would keep track of it, down to the last lira and piaster. If a colleague or friend had made him the same offer, or a relative had done it—she asked him—would he have turned it down? He said nothing. And she decided his silence meant one thing. "So, you despise my tainted money, just like you despise me? I knew it. You don't object in principle, but you won't take the loan from me? Is that it?" Her reproach was full of pain.

Did he weaken in the face of her pleading? And did he eventually accept because he intended to pay her back, or had circumstances given him no choice? All he knew was that he had accepted.

Every lira he received was recorded in a small notebook he carried, and he would return them to her piaster by piaster. She could rest assured that he was not taking advantage of a weak female. A woman from the brothels? Yes, but she had more humanity in her than any of those men at the ceremony who had made sure to leave an empty seat between her and them—those men who would jump at the chance to devour her in private.

Wasn't he doing the same?

Why had he failed to give her an invitation?

Wasn't it just another way of leaving an empty seat between them, to convince the people around him that he came from one world and she from another?

Was he afraid of being embarrassed in front of his friends if they found out that she held a favor over him? He had planned to sneak off to visit her after the ceremony; he would allow her to give him a congratulatory kiss, and perhaps return it with two of his own. Brandishing his little notebook, he planned to say, "You've spent this much on me, and you can count on me to pay it back in installments within six months."

Hadn't he intended to speak to her in words that dripped with gratitude? Hadn't he, in fact, planned to erase her shame by saying, "You are the most honorable person I know"?

Indeed, he should have done that and more. But for her to come here, inviting sly winks from his friends? For him to be forced to endure his colleague's nudges, and then watch as more nudges traveled down the line? For all those eyes to attack him, full of unbearable accusations? That could not be tolerated.

Some of his friends knew about the two of them, but nobody knew their relationship was different from the typical arrangement between buyer and seller, between all those who sold and all those who bought.

Why had that madwoman come here? Didn't she know this was the last place she should have intruded on? How he hated her, hated the circumstances that had forced him to turn to her! How despicable he had been to accept, and how despicable she had been to come and flaunt what she'd done for him.

More and more sweat dripped from his forehead, but his limbs were freezing, and growing stiff from the cold.

The line he was standing in moved toward the left side of the platform. Oh God, in a few minutes, it would be his turn. Would that foolish woman give him away with her clapping? Would it make all the heads turn and draw a thousand question marks in people's eyes? He could see her from where he stood on the left side of the platform, but he was trying not to let her know that he'd spotted her.

Three, two, one... There was only one person in front of him now. And then they called his name.

He stepped forward, holding out an icy hand for the dean to shake, accepting the certificate with his other hand, then quickly climbing down the far side of the stage. Perhaps by moving so fast, he could leave room for confusion between people's clapping for the next person and her clapping for him. He forgot, in his fluster, to turn the tassel to the right as they had taught him, so he could become an official graduate, and his colleagues' voices rose up, alerting him to his mistake. When he stood to adjust the tassel, his gaze instinctively jumped in her direction, and he caught sight of her as she got up and slipped through the rows, alone except for the looks that followed her. She hadn't bothered to stay and congratulate him, nor to make sure he'd noticed she was there. Not troubling herself with convention, she didn't even wait until the ceremony was over and the guests had begun to disperse.

HER STORY

My Dearest Brother,

I wish I was still unknown to you. I wanted you to carry on as you were, without a sister whose existence tortures you so much that the mere mention of her name makes you hang your head in shame, wishing she had never been born. But I saw you a few days ago. You were walking through our neighborhood, your footsteps stumbling, anxious, confused. I recognized your face—it's still the same—and I read it from a distance. It told me what I had been expecting, and I knew that my "news" must have reached you. I was sure that the spiteful Awad hadn't left you in peace and that he'd told you my story…

Perhaps he used it to humiliate you. Maybe he went too far, slicing your feelings, goading you until the blood rushed to your head, and you were robbed of sleep that night and the nights that followed. Maybe you went hungry for a week—or weeks—to save up for a gun so you could empty it into my head when we next meet. I knew my instincts had been right when I saw your fingers tighten around something in your pocket.

It was the gun. No doubt about it.

Yes, I expected all this when you left the orphanage where you'd spent your youth. You became a fine young man, pure of heart, soul, and gaze, who worked hard to make an honest living. You needed a place to live, somewhere to call home and keep your meager belongings, but the only place you could find was in our old alley, where we lived when our father was alive. That was when I was overcome by a sense of foreboding. I knew Awad wouldn't leave you alone until he had filled your head with my story. Because of course, our neighborhood has its honor to consider, and it looks down on such things. There's a stain that must be erased. And, on top of that, the men need a tale to amuse them as they sit around their cups of black tea at the coffeehouse, and the women need fresh topics for their gossiping tongues when they lean their heads out of the window or gather at a neighbors' house. And a juicy story like mine is guaranteed to entertain the neighborhood for months on end.

My poor brother. I don't pity myself because of your foolish bullets; they would relieve me of so many things, and put an end to this existence that I vomit up every second of the day. It would soothe the nerves deadened by the cheap dirty emotions of every pig with a pocketful of coins who wants to buy memories of a red-hot night.

No, I don't pity myself as much as I pity you, and this is the only pure emotion in my heart. I grieve for your innocent youth, spent suffocating between slimy prison walls.

Did Awad say anything besides "kill her"? Did he tell you our story? The story of the day our father died and left the two of us children behind? I was fourteen and you were five. The neighborhood women cried crocodile tears over him and thanked God that he had laid his wife to rest first, "so she wouldn't have to drink down the pain of this loss." The men agreed about their duty to the dead, but fled from any mercy for the living. Did he tell you how he approached me the next day? I already hated him because once, he had tried to force a kiss on me. I complained to our father about it, and he'd walked up to Awad at his coffee shop and spat in his horrible face, then cursed him to hell. Well, when Awad showed up offering his services, I firmly turned him away. I refused the coins he held out, and I wouldn't let him cross the doorstep.

Did he tell you the story of a girl who had no one to take her hand in a huge, lonely world, where with every step of her little foot, she feared she would stumble? Then let me tell it. Yes, let me. The accused has a right to speak before her neck ends up in the noose of public opinion. We were young, my brother, and all we had was a poverty that tore our bodies with its fangs, so I went looking for a job that my small hands could manage. I asked and pleaded and coaxed until I ended up in a sewing factory. The owner met me and said, "Show me your hands."

I spread out my hands, and he said, "Oh, you have slender fingers. No doubt you'll do well. Go and see the lead girl, and she'll show you the work. If you do a good job, I'll give you five piasters a day."

I turned to head over to the lead girl, and then I heard him saying, "Did you know you have a beautiful face, girl?"

I hadn't known, until then, that I had a beautiful face! After, I found myself in a crowd of girls, all of them thin and pallid, their young backs bent over the looms, their fingers on autopilot.

I copied them, and I copied them well. And I earned the five piasters, with a smile on top from the pot-bellied factory owner—a smile I didn't understand.

I worked all day long, leaving you in the care of Umm Mahmoud, the only kind woman in the neighborhood. I would come back to you in the evenings, my hands full of bread, olives, and cheese, and my heart full of eagerness and longing. I would rush home, deterred by nothing except the hateful specter of Awad; he would buttonhole me sometimes, in dark alleyways, and I would rain insults on him and then run off, driven by rage, fear, and dread.

I was hard-working, so my pay jumped from five to eight and then ten piasters… This made the girls resentful, and they began to wag their tongues behind my back. I thought I heard them say, "We've been expecting this since the day she showed up. She has a pretty face, light skin, and green eyes. Don't you see him eating her up with his eyes?"

I didn't like their attacks, and I didn't know if the "master"—as we called him—was eating me up with his eyes, as they claimed. He was nice to me, and I put his niceness down to some sort of kindness and compassion. As for the raise, I deserved it. One day, he came to inspect the work, wandering between the rows of employees. When he got to me, he patted my shoulder and said, "Why don't you stay for a while after the others leave. I'd like to have a word with you."

I spent the rest of my day thinking about what he might want from me. A tremor raced through me, ripping away my peace of mind. When it was time to go, I tried to slip out with the others, but I saw the master at the door. He signaled for me to wait, so I fell behind. As soon as the place was empty, he pulled me by the hand into his office, opened a drawer, and took out a bottle of perfume and a bracelet made from colored beads. "These are for you," he said. "I'm happy with your work, so take them."

I didn't reach out a hand, so he pulled me closer, but I managed to wriggle away like a little cat. I escaped to the road through the open door, my heart gripped by a powerful fear of something mysterious and unknown. At the bend in the road, I saw Awad, looking at me with his hateful face and his plastic smile. Maybe he'd been waiting for me. Maybe he'd asked the other girls what happened when he noticed I was late. As soon as he saw me, he said, "I wonder why the manager kept you back, of all the girls. Did he…? I expected this would happen, you—" and then out shot a filthy word that shook my tender being to the core, so I ran back to you, terrified and crying. You looked at me with confused eyes, and then you burst out crying with me. We slept next to each other, and I pulled your little body close, as if hoping you could protect me from the master, from Awad, from other people, and from the feelings that stormed my heart.

I didn't go to work the next day. I wanted to stay safe by your side. But—worn down by Umm Mahmoud's pestering questions about why I'd stopped going—I found myself forced to return. So I went, and the Master noticed me coming in; he gave a foxlike smile and meaningful nod.

That evening, he had a "word" with me, and the following evenings, he had "words." I heard promises from him about dresses, perfumes, candy—everything that could turn a deprived girl's head. But I couldn't stand being with him. My little heart would pound in terror, and I never felt at ease. And I hated him even more when he brought his greedy lips to my cheek and started kissing me, paying no attention to the slaps I showered onto his fat face. As soon as he let me go, I ran like the wind, intending never to show my face there again. I stayed away for a few days, but then I hung my head and went back—because we were hungry. I had tried to find another job, and I even went to work in service for a family. But I left, thanks to the onslaught of slaps that fell on me from the cruel mistress of the house as a punishment for breaking two glasses. I didn't even ask for my pay for the week I'd worked for her. There was no escape. I had to go back to the looms.

The game of cat and mouse between me and the master went on for a long time. My nerves suffered, worn down by the length of the chase. Then the prey fell—once—and soon after that, she was cast aside. The bastard threw her out, her dignity wounded, her pride stripped away. Terrified, confused, crying, broken, racked by malice, and hounded by contempt everywhere she went.

This time, I couldn't go home or back to the neighborhood. Awad's gossip had preceded me, along with the venom he spewed in every corner with his tales. Lips moved—not to find excuses or justifications, or to ask God for His protection—but to curse me and rip me to shreds.

I wandered aimlessly for days. And with every day that passed, my belief in life's justice died a little more. Eventually, I found myself in a black hellhole that swallowed a new victim every day and went on asking for more.

There, I learned to forge my humanity in a bitter crucible. I learned to hate, I learned to take revenge—and I learned other things, so many things. I became a real professional!

I would emerge sometimes, from the depths of this immense bitterness, and think about you, and then I'd break down and cry. I sent someone to bring me your news and learned that you had ended up in an orphanage after Umm Mahmoud begged and pressured the neighborhood mayor to do something for this wretched child—who was you. My longing tortured me again, and I made up my mind to see you, bringing some presents with me. But when I arrived, I stood in confusion in front of the closed door. I didn't know how to get in, or what to say, or who to ask for, so I threw the parcel I was carrying in through the window and left without a backward glance.

After that, ties between our two worlds were cut. I think you probably asked about me now and again, and missed me a little and then a lot, but when longing for me didn't do you any good, your memory of me fell dormant. The days flipped past, and my image disappeared from your mind. I forgive, you were young.

As for me—also young, but old beyond my years—I didn't forget you, and I continued to scavenge for news of you. My love for you is the only connection between me and the world of emotions. Apart from that, storms of loathing eat away at my heart.

Once again, I say that I pity that, having just reached manhood, you would sell your life so cheaply. And again I say, May God protect you from the company of a vile man like Awad, whom I hated in the innocence of my childhood, and whom I spurned even when I was broken-winged and defenseless. When once, he knocked at my door with the others who came knocking, I rose up from the depths of my mire to snub him. I slammed my open door in his face and sent him off with a flood of curses.

Take that stupid gun and sell it, little one. Buy yourself a shirt to cover your bare shoulders instead of that torn one. You haven't taken it off in the whole two weeks you've spent spying on our alley, ever since the idea of revenge dragged you here… to your sister.

NIGHT VISIONS

She shook off the covers, begging for the strength to drive off the dark fingers of pain that dug into her soul, tearing at the peace in her young heart and hounding her with attacks from that nightmarish vision.

But it was no use fighting against the vision. The face still hovered in front of her, and in front of her alone: her roommates were fast asleep, as proven by the snores that kept her from suffering in peace. It was as if the nightmare had plotted against her in particular, claiming her night's rest as its victim.

Suddenly she hated those girls, hated their faces, hated their rigid features that showed neither happiness nor pain.

And she couldn't bear the darkness that hid the outlines of the big hall, where more than twenty beds were set out in neat rows. The orphans lay in a regimented silence, undisturbed by a single murmur, not even when the matron came to switch off the lights, ordering them to sleep, "Right now!"

She sat up in bed, trying to challenge the image, but it refused to be erased. It didn't disappear for a second, and her gaze remained fixed on the waxen face with its mouth stuffed with cotton and its glass eyes half-open.

She hadn't known until today that death could be ugly. Repulsive. Terrible. No—her mother's face hadn't really looked like that; her mother's face had felt familiar, as if her mother had been about to smile, about to part her lips to soothe her daughter's tears.

How beautiful her mother had been, even in death!

That morning, she'd been busy helping out with the breakfast dishes, washing off the streaks of leftover grape molasses, when one of her fellow orphans came over and flatly announced that the orphans had been invited to a funeral. She didn't understand what that meant until right before lunch. The girls had been standing around the long wooden tables, saying a prayer undermined by hunger—a prayer from which she understood nothing, even though it was repeated several times a day—when a teacher came to tell them to eat quickly so they could make it to the funeral on time. Only then did she dare ask someone sitting next to her about it. Shoving a spoonful of soup into her large mouth, the girl told her that a rich man had died, and that his family had invited the orphans to mourn at his funeral.

Her neighbor had said nothing more, and she stopped asking questions, since she could see the girl was busy tearing into the dark bread, destroying its perfect roundness.

And after lunch, when she saw the others taking their empty plates to the kitchen, wiped as clean as if they'd been washed, she had done the same and then followed them to another room. There, for the first time, she had put on her blue pinafore—it was too long, but the teacher said she'd grow into it in a year or two. She pinned the orphanage badge to her uniform, squeezed her neck into a starched collar, and put on thick-soled shoes. Then she'd moved to the edge of the room and waited to see what would happen next. Eventually, the teacher arrived and told them to line up on the playground, where they stood for twenty minutes, and then set off…

On the way, she had made no attempt to raise her head—the teacher had said not to—but she heard people talking, when they saw the somber blue procession, wondering about who had died. And so she understood that the girls never set foot outside the big door's threshold unless death was involved.

Now, after having settled back in bed, she sat up abruptly, holding her palms over her ears to block out the thin screams the dead man's family had let out when the girls came in, screams that had squeezed her heart and drowned her face in tears. Digging her heels in, she'd hesitated, not wanting to go inside. She didn't even know how to say a prayer.

But the teacher had nudged her, indicating, with the tip of her finger, that she should stand with the others around the dead man—after all, that's why they were there. Her place was by the head. It was an ugly picture of death, and the dozens of flowers spread all around did nothing to soften its cruelty. When her mother died, there had been only a single red rose that she'd picked from the lone flowerpot on their balcony and laid on her mother's chest. That chest had been warm, and she'd thought she could feel a heart still beating, so she refused to believe her mother could die. Her father was dead, it was true, but she hadn't known him. In her mind, it made sense that fathers might die. As for her mother…

But today, she had gotten to know death, and its smells and sights filled her: incense, flowers, and the pungent scent of bodies exhausted by a tumult of emotions. There were two candles with dwindling flames: one at the corpse's head, the other at its feet. A cold, open-lidded coffin in the corner of the room. And a waxen yellow face with glass eyes and a mouth stuffed with cotton.

Dragging the pillow from under her head, she pressed it into her eyes, trying to banish the image for a few moments. It was horrible to spend the night in front of that face, which vied with her mother's. She wished she could see her mother's face instead, since she was always full of laughter and tenderness when she appeared. Once, her mother had kissed her and given her something, but by morning she had forgotten what it was. Another time, she had sat by her side, talking to her so naturally that she had gotten up to look for her, convinced that her mother had come back to life. She didn't think of it as a miracle—she had often heard stories about people who'd been thought dead and buried alive—but when she confessed her night visions to her grandmother, the old woman crossed herself, saying, "My dear, your mother's no Christ! Next time, if she visits at night, say a prayer for her soul."

So her mother's death was a truth, then, and it couldn't be changed by visiting ghosts. And even those visits had stopped since she'd arrived at the orphanage: her mother's soul didn't wander in unfamiliar places, otherwise she would have visited her tonight to rid her of this image that weighed so heavily on her spirit, plucking the tranquility from her young heart.

Her head stayed under the pillow for who knows how long, but she finally fell asleep, only to open her eyes to the unsmiling face of her large-mouthed neighbor, who said, "Get up! We get up at six, and the other girls are almost done making their beds."

So she got up and shook out her sheets, spreading them back on her bed before going to splash her face with water and then joining the line to the dining room. There she sat, gazing into space, not touching the molasses or the olives. And then it occurred to her to ask: "Does the orphanage always go to funerals?"

Her neighbor spoke through a huge wad of food. "Two or three times a week, maybe more. We go whenever we're invited because the management charges money for it. How else would they pay our bills? Eat, eat—don't you like molasses? Well, give me your share if you're not hungry, give it!"

THE IRONING MAN'S APPRENTICE

"You've got half an hour to sweep the floor, clean the ashes out of the iron, and fill it up with coal again. Then you have to turn off the light and go to sleep."

"Okay, boss."

"And the light, remember. Don't fall asleep with the light on. I'm going to walk past here a little later, and if—"

"Okay, boss, okay."

"And don't you dare take the customers' clothes and use them to cover yourself, or else—"

Rizq didn't let his boss, Aram the ironing man, finish his sentence; he blurted out ten "okay bosses" in a row, his lips pulled back in an unreadable smile.

Aram closed the door and secured it with a heavy piece of metal before he pulled on his faded beret and set off, leaving Rizq, with his meaningless smile, to run a threadbare broom around the corners of the shop, gathering the sweepings into a pile that he was going to let sit until morning. Afterwards, finally taking a breath, Rizq reached into his pocket, emptying it of paper bills and small change. A quarter of a lira from Ustaz Khalil. Five piasters from Madame Elaine, who owned the boarding house—yes, a measly five piasters: women were not generous with him. Plus ten from the student who stayed in one of her rooms. As for the rest, they hadn't given him anything.

Forty piasters in takings for a long day's work! It didn't matter: at least the money would stay in his pocket, since he'd forgotten to buy a loaf of bread and some falafel before Aram locked him in.

Well, it wouldn't be hard to go without supper tonight—he'd had rice for lunch! While delivering a gentleman's suit, he'd come across the housemaid, about to empty a plate of rice into the bin that waited at the door for the garbage collector.

Astonished to see her wasting a big plateful of food, Rizq had given her a puzzled look. Sensing his longing, she'd asked if he would like to eat it. He was hungry, so he wasn't ashamed to say yes. He'd eaten the rice and found it delicious, especially when the maid brought him some leftover broth with white beans swimming in it. As he ate, he'd tried to remember the last time he'd had rice, deciding it had been back in the mountains, before he ran away from his brother and vicious sister-in-law.

Stuffing the paper bills into the cloth bag he kept tied to his waist, Rizq walked over to the cardboard box that had once held a radio set, which he now used to store his meager belongings. From there, he took out a suit he'd bought for a whole lira at the hawker's market, intending to use it as bedding. He spread it out near the door, where noises that leaked in through the crack would keep him company: the footsteps of passersby, or the radio from the nearby falafel store—Fairouz might even sing him his favorite song, "Hayk Mashe' el-Zaaroura."

The customers' suits that Aram's iron had glided over were lined up on a rope strung between two nails on opposite walls; they hung there in a row, having drained the sweat out of Aram as he toiled to get them neat and clean. With his back bent over the iron, Aram cut a truly pitiful figure. Rizq had watched him for a long time that afternoon as he repeatedly wiped his face and bald spot with a khaki handkerchief, then lifted the earthenware jug to his mouth to drink, giving Rizq the impression that the water went into his belly and instantly came back out again, gathering in shiny drops on his ancient bald head.

After some hesitation, Rizq suggested that Aram should let him practice with the iron so he could make himself useful in the shop. Raising his sweaty face, Aram had said, in a voice that still retained its Armenian lilt, "Why? To turn you into a muallim, a master who'll open his own laundry to compete with mine?"

Rizq had been slightly alarmed when Aram then let go of the big metal iron and came up to him, seizing him by the hand and dragging him to the laundry door, saying, "Look. That's Abdullah, he used to work for me. And that's Mahmoud, and over there's a third one who opened a shop on Hamra Street. I poured all my energy into teaching them, and then, when they got the knack of it, they lured my customers away... No! Aram won't make the same mistake again. I'm not going to make you into a new muallim; you'll keep on delivering clothes to the customers and getting your ten lira at the end of the month. Got it? I'm no donkey!"

And he went and picked up the iron again, running it irritably over the shirt, repeating, "Aram is not a donkey, Aram is not a donkey..."

Rizq could find no justification for all this anger; he had suggested that Aram teach him to iron out of pity—not with any particular motive in mind.

But when he lay down for the night on his bedding, after having grown tired of listening to passing footsteps and deciding which were men's and which were women's, and after Saeed had closed his falafel store, cutting off the sound of the radio, Rizq wasn't afraid to think about his right to become a muallim.

Becoming a muallim was far from easy. The heat that radiated off the iron melted his flesh, but to him, that was still better than running errands by which Aram set no store. In Aram's opinion, the errands weren't real work, so every time he gave Rizq his ten lira at the end of the month, or a few days into the new month, he'd say, "Here. You don't deserve it. What do you do in return for all that money? When I worked in a shop, I didn't cost my boss more than five lira a month. And he had a temper and beat me if he got angry. And I didn't get paid baksheesh like you do. You're a good-for-nothing, but you still take ten lira a month from me, a hundred and twenty a year, six hundred in five years, and then one day you'll go open a shop and take up the trade. Oh yes—you won't be any better than the others."

And he'd turn his head to spit as he gave Rizq a ten-lira note with tattered, filthy edges.

While Rizq was thinking, a long time went by. He heard the diner door closing, and then the grilled-corn-on-the-cob vendor also dragged his cart away. After that, silence reigned, except when the tram's metal wheels trundled over the tracks, and the laundry's door shook from the vibrations.

His throat felt dry, so he got up to drink from the earthenware jug, tilting it so he could suck at its mouth. He wished he could switch on the light to keep him company, but, afraid of Aram's surprises, he forced himself back to bed, trying to catch any sound from the street that might make the muted night more companionable.

But he soon got caught up in his thoughts and allowed himself to imagine his hand wielding an iron over pliant American shirts, white jackets, and khaki pants—but no dresses. He didn't dare tackle dresses, because ironing them was a complicated process that exhausted even Aram himself. But he would conquer them when he became a muallim.

Yes, he had decided to become a muallim.

Getting up again, he hesitated before turning on the light, afraid it might shine through the gap beneath the door, or leak out of the small inside window that looked out onto a garage that was closed for the night. But he overcame his doubts, reaching out and confidently flipping the switch, flooding the place with light so it looked to him exactly as it did during the day: everything was the same except for Aram, who wasn't standing in front of the ironing board with the iron in his right hand and the damp khaki handkerchief in his left.

The iron was waiting for Rizq, already full of coal. So, before indecision could cripple his will, he poured on a little kerosene, and then held a match close to the iron, triggering a burst of demonic flames. He rushed to turn off the light so he could savor the sight of the fiery red tongues as they cast flickering shadows onto the piles of clothes. There was a surprising variety of garments, belonging to people of different shapes, sizes, and temperaments—people from disparate walks of life.

But the laundry had brought their clothes together.

The flames began to die down, and the place grew dark again, meaning he had to turn the light back on so he could begin his experiment. But what to start with? He couldn't decide.

Then he caught sight of a colorful shirt, one of three he had brought back to be laundered from Ustaz Khalil's room. He decided to start with the colorful one, since it wouldn't show any burn marks. Anyway, it would be good to do something for Ustaz Khalil, since he was the kindest person Rizq delivered clothes to. Only yesterday, the Ustaz had been standing in front of a store, buying the stuff that's a bit like dondurma—what children called "merry cream." And when Rizq walked by, the Ustaz had called him over and asked the seller to give him one, paying for it out of his own pocket. Sticking out his tongue, Rizq had taken a gentle lick to explore its taste, but when he carried it into the laundry, there was no escape from Aram's tongue: he had asked Rizq to let him taste it, and then proceeded to wolf down the white dome that nestled on top of the cone, finishing it off completely.

Rizq picked up the shirt and spread it out on the ironing board, smiling as he thought about how, in the morning, Aram would think he was the one who had ironed it. But Rizq wasn't going to deceive Ustaz Khalil—he would tell him that he had ironed it himself.

Filled with elation and a teasing sense of anxiety, Rizq lifted the iron, then put it down for a moment on the sleeve before he quickly picked it up again.

Little by little, the fabric flattened under his iron, and the black squares adorning the red shirt straightened, emboldening him to rest the full weight of the iron on the sleeve, dragging it repeatedly back and forth. When he waited a few moments before lifting it, he found that a piece of sleeve had stuck to the iron, causing his eyes to nearly pop from his head.

The shirt was burnt! Ustaz Khalil's shirt! His favorite customer's shirt! The man who never once saw him without giving him something.

Rizq's fingers froze around the iron. What would Aram do to him tomorrow? He was going to kill him! Bring the whole world down on his head! If only he could escape, if only he could push through that locked door and run, run to somewhere Aram and his sweaty yellow fingers couldn't reach him.

He should have stayed where he belonged instead of dreaming about ironed shirts and earning the title of "muallim."

He wished he had burned anything but the Ustaz's shirt. What would he say to Aram? What a storm Aram would kick up in the morning! But he wouldn't mind bearing the brunt of Aram's outburst, if only the shirt hadn't been burnt. What would the Ustaz say?

Would he scowl at him for the first time ever? If he knew where the Ustaz had gotten his shirt, he would have gone there now and bought a new one for him, even if he had to pay every lira he owned.

If only that door would open, if that door would just open up... Rizq's tears poured down his cheeks as he crumpled to the floor, his head resting against the door, wishing that morning would never come. Exhausted from crying and racking his brains, he finally surrendered his head to the rags he had made into a pillow and dreamed a dream in which he saw the shirt—the shirt with the burnt sleeve—and Aram, with his bony face and faded beret, raining curses on his fathers and grandfathers. But he wasn't afraid because, in his dream, he had seen Ustaz Khalil smiling at him and calming his fears, saying, "Don't you worry about that shirt, Rizq, what really matters is that you tried to become a muallim."

THE BICYCLE PUMP

I couldn't think of a better distraction from the heavy, dreary boredom plaguing me than catching the six o'clock show at the local cinema, which audiences called the "matinee."

There were only a few people in the spacious hall, most of them high-school students. I found myself a seat, and before long the show began. My eyes glued themselves to the screen, which was playing one of those half-baked movies that only people with questionable artistic taste enjoy. Halfway through, I was already fed up with it, even though I had gone in with low expectations; cinemas here usually save the stronger movies for the weekend, when they can be sure to attract a bigger audience, while the weekday movie-goers are looking for something—anything—to kill time. Unable to sit through till the end, I decided to leave without giving any thought to where I'd go next. I snuck out the door and found the world wrapped in twilight, calling for help from the streetlights to keep the darkness at bay. Bicycles are the only way to get around in this town, and I was looking for my bike among the others leaning against the wall when I saw a boy bending over one of its wheels. He was fiddling with the cap on the valve, and I watched as the tire went flat with a loud exhalation.

The boy was startled when my large hand came down on his shoulder, but he didn't dare raise his head to look at me. I yanked at him and, as he stood up, I got a look at his dirty, grease-streaked face. It was the boy who worked at the nearby bike-repair shop. It dawned on me then that this might not be the first time he'd tampered with my bike. I remembered that I'd heard from some friends about how they too had found their bikes—which they'd left outside the club, or the cinema, or their homes—with the air let out of their tires, making them impossible to ride. It made sense from the boy's point of view: he'd creep around meddling with the tires, letting out the air, so that, when we got out of the cinema, we'd have to head for the workshop to pump them up, and he'd get our money the easy way.

Exasperated, I pressed down harder on his shoulder. "So it's you," I said. "Nice work."

Panicked, the boy looked left and right, and a cold sweat broke out on his shiny yellow forehead.

"Let me go, Sir. I swear I—"

"You what? I caught you at it myself."

"I... Oh, you won't understand if I tell you."

"What could you possibly say to excuse such criminal behavior?"

Jerking away, he seized my hand and shoved it off his shoulder, saying, "Don't make up your mind so fast. I'm not a criminal. Let me go, for God's sake. Don't you understand?"

Tears washed his eyes, and I felt my anger transform into uncertainty as he begged me not to report him to the police and promised to pump up the tire for free. Eager to get rid of me, he didn't wait to hear my answer, but went to get my bike and walked it to his shop. There, he quickly took out his big pump and filled up the tires, then passed a rag over the bike, wiping off the dust. Finally, he pushed it toward me, that trembling look peeping out of his eyes.

I smiled a little to take the edge off his fear, and he grew more relaxed, saying, "If you come by every day, I'll take care of your bike for free."

My smile grew wider, relieving more of his worries. He dared to ask, "Are you going to turn me in?"

In fact, the thought of reporting the incident to the police hadn't even crossed my mind. To a peace-lover like me, it was too trivial a matter to warrant going to the station and getting embroiled in endless debates, especially since the authorities here focused too much on minor cases. Otherwise, they didn't have enough important stuff going on to keep their men busy. So, as I got ready to climb onto my bike, I said, "No, provided there's no more nonsense like this in future."

I turned my bike toward the road that led to my house, but I had gone only a short way when I noticed the boy following me on his bicycle. With a single move, he cut me off and blocked my way, stumbling over his words as he said, "Sir, this road leads to the police station, and you promised me—"

"And I'm keeping my word," I interrupted sharply.

"Thank you." The boy said it slowly, searching my eyes before he started to turn back. But he hesitated. "I want to tell you something, but I'm afraid you won't listen." He looked left and right, then continued, "And in any case, this isn't the place..."

I don't know what made me go along with the boy's wishes, but I was drawn to him by a kind of pity. "Come with me," I said, then took him to a nearby café. I led him to a corner table and ordered him a cold drink.

Perhaps he sensed my questioning gaze on his face, because he looked down and began nervously to play with his fingers.

I interrupted his uncertain silence, asking, "So what did you want to say?"

"Nothing. I just wanted to ask, do you think I'm a criminal?"

I couldn't think of a calm, sensible answer to give him.

"I can practically read your mind," he said. "And it's your right, Sir, to despise someone like me. I know what I did is shameful, but—"

"But what?"

"I have a mother, and a sister and brother who live by my mother's needle, and by what I make from pumping up bike tires. At the repair shop, I work for a few piasters until five in the evening, and then the boss goes home and leaves the shop to me. And that's my only chance to make a little money to live on. I feel so ashamed when I hear the lessons at night school, encouraging us to be honest and upright, and then I find myself forced to act like this during the day. Even my God-fearing mother doesn't know the secret behind these piasters I bring home: she'd never take the money if she did. I was lucky it was a kind person like you who caught me, otherwise I'd have been locked up. But isn't it miserable that I can't promise you I'll stop this terrible behavior, unless I choose a life of hunger for myself and for my family?"

The boy stopped talking, strangled by his tears, so I patted his shoulder comfortingly and guided him out. And before we parted at the café's door, he took my hand in his to shake it, and held out some coins in his other. "You don't deserve it that I took your money," he said. "Take these back. I've seen you more than once, waiting your turn to pump up the tires on your bike."

I didn't know what to say. All I did was to curse the world, then take out all the coins I had in my pocket and push them on him. Then I turned my face away, afraid to meet the eyes that were full of wounded pride.

I WANT WATER

The familiar tap of light footsteps and the swish of a loose black habit echoed through the room, prompting dancing eyes to shutter and bodies to stretch out in affected repose. Some cunning girls overplayed their hand, letting out snores that didn't fool Sister Marta for one second. She quietened them by shaking their beds until all was still and only the sound of silence could be heard—that, and the sound of a single head flipping back and forth on its pillow. Every time her tired head turned to the right, the pillow would press down against the envelope beneath, and she'd hear an ominous rustling as the letter's words stabbed at her head. The prayer on her lips faded away, washed into the quilt by two lines of tears.

The quilt knew her secret: her prayers and supplications had given her away, and so had the long black rosary, its beads hurtling past her thumb and forefinger, as if in a race against Sin. She was paying for the sin with this anxiety that pricked her conscience and ate away at the security of a childhood she had left behind only two months before. The sin had cost her more than the worth of her whole life, a worth announced by this letter that refused to settle for anything less, spurning the penalties she was used to paying for her transgressions. Her punishment for trying to cheat, for example, or for breaking a rule, would be the loss of a necklace, or the slip of a foot on rough ground. She knew there was a price for everything, and she had spent the last week waiting for a judgment for this sin. She'd begged for help from every pale statue that stood in a corner of the church, but not one of them had batted an eyelid. Nor did the ten candles intercede for her, even though she had humbled herself before them. They had all abandoned her, for what mercy awaits someone who lies to God?

What a misery it is to be born female! Is there no way to mark womanhood but the flood? This red flood that Sister Marta said she should expect every three weeks, which brought on all the pain in her stomach, her back, and her knees, making her light-headed and sick. She was barely able to sit or sleep for fear of being given away by a tiny stain that would hand her schoolmates a chance to come at her with snide remarks, like the ones they'd made when it happened the first time, two months ago. It had taken her by surprise, and she hadn't been prepared or known what to do; she hadn't even realized it had anything to do with the cramps that had stopped her from joining a game until Salwa—and, out of all her friends, it had to be sharp-tongued Salwa—surprised her by grabbing the hem of her dress from behind, announcing, "I think you'd better show this to Sister Marta. She'll tell you you're not a little girl anymore."

Salwa had let out a laugh that sent the blood rushing to her face, and she'd fled, moving awkwardly toward the bathroom nearest the playground, where she'd discovered this shameful thing. After half an hour spent in agony, she came out to the sound of Salwa and her gang pounding on the door, their curiosity piqued by this extraordinary discovery.

She had wished the earth would open up and swallow her, since that would have been easier to bear than what she heard, "Leave her alone girls, she's a woman now!"

How that thought terrified her! She had been trying to slow it down: wearing loose clothes to hide the swellings on her chest, not letting her mother know about them when she went home on vacation. She wished now that she had told her mother, back then, since maybe that admission would have paved the way to a talk about this thing that had come upon her out of the blue, giving her no clue to when it might start, nor end, nor how to be prepared for it.

She had always wondered why the older girls weren't ashamed of their breasts, and how they didn't think twice about drawing attention to them with tight-fitting clothes. As for her, she hated nothing more than being told she was "all grown up now" or "a real young lady, ready for marriage" or any other of the descriptions favored by her mother's friends who—every time they saw her at home on a school break—would lean over to ask her mother something in a voice too low for her to hear. But she always heard the same answer, "Not yet."

Now, her mother would say, "Yes," and she would be mortified at her mother's words.

It was the truth, though, no matter how hard she tried to hide it. She should have gotten used to it, accepted it—never mind the pain it had caused her and the hurtful comments that had come her way—and then she wouldn't have complained about it, even to God, nor paid this steep price. A lost necklace or a knee scraped in a fall were much easier to bear than this illness of Farid's, the only son among three daughters. She knew what Farid meant to her parents, and to every spinster and old woman in the family. She hadn't understood how much having a son meant to a family until her aunt flung open the door of the room where her mother had given birth and trilled out a zaghrouda, and she saw a sheep being slaughtered on their doorstep. Her grandmother's face had broken into a laugh so wide her generous mouth could hardly contain it, and she began touching her hand to the ground, then back to her forehead in thanks.

The house had buzzed with the clamor of well-wishing women, and pots of celebratory meghli pudding had bubbled on the stove. Meanwhile, she had gone, after her aunt's prodding, to congratulate her mother, uncertain whether to love or hate the lump of bluish flesh that later became Farid.

And now Farid was sick, according to the letter.

Everyone—her father, her mother, the doctor—would wonder why, but only she would know. She alone would know that a major penance was needed to pay for her sin. For He did not just visit the sins of the fathers on their children, as the Sister taught them in religion lessons; He also visited the sins of siblings on one another. It was no small thing to trick God, even though she had acted in good faith when the flood visited her the second time. No, it hadn't been a trick. It couldn't have been. She had been embarrassed to make an excuse that excluded her from taking Communion. She hadn't even known this thing had anything to do with one of the church's sacred mysteries, but a friend had warned her not to do it unless she was pure and clean—even going near the altar in her condition was considered a major sin. She was tormented by the thought of such a disclosure; it would give Salwa another chance to taunt and shame her for being a woman. Can you imagine? A woman! She refused to use that to excuse herself. She had knelt for a long time in front of her bed, barely sleeping for three nights as she pleaded with God for it to end before Sunday. And on Sunday morning, she'd thought that Heaven had been more merciful than Salwa's mockery, when it seemed that she would be able to approach the divine mystery. So she answered her older friend's question confidently, "Yes, I can."

And she hadn't thought she was lying: in church, she felt a load had been lifted from her shoulders. But two hours later, she realized her mistake. Stunned, she'd felt her limbs stiffen. Her throat had gone dry, and her eyes were suddenly burning, on fire. How could she have done this? How could she have lied to God? What punishment did she deserve? What torment?

Wasn't it torment enough that her head was consumed by these buzzing thoughts? Your brother's going to die... die... die! Yes, die. And you will be saved, you who lied to God. Your mother will wear black, and your father will weep tears of red blood as he bids farewell to a small rosewood coffin, covered in flowers of every color. The family will be left with no son, and the miserable sisters with no brother.

Her tears conjured up an image of the coffin. If there must be a coffin, then let it be a bigger one, with her lying in it; let it be lifted and carried away, unadorned, to the sound of hymns sung by schoolgirls in white collars. Would she die if she threw herself out the window? She'd wait until morning to do it. But why not now? Was she worried about disturbing the slumbering girls? Why should she care about them, when she was the one who was going to be dead? Look at that Salwa, sleeping like a stupid cow. It was all her fault, and yet there she was, fast asleep, with her hateful snores growing louder and louder. Salwa would gloat over her torn and twisted body... No! She wouldn't give Salwa the satisfaction of seeing her as a head missing a body, or as a body missing a leg. She would die by poison, by anything she could use as poison. If she was at home, she would have swallowed the red pellets of rat poison her father scattered on the storeroom floor. But she was here, so how could she do it? Even death seemed meager in this place. Oh yes, she could take Aspro! Some people killed themselves with it, and she had an entire box in her locker—she'd taken only one pill so far, for her cramps. And the locker was unlocked. She'd get up now; if she put off death, she'd lose her chance. But what if the locker was locked? Wouldn't the grating of the key in the lock wake one of the sleeping girls?

But no, it was open. Everything was in place for her to do the deed. Damn them, these heartless cows! Wasn't there a single one of them who felt her pain, who sensed she was about to die, alone, without anyone saying "no" to her? Without Mona waking up or—or even Salwa?

Here was the box. If she swallowed every last pill, she'd die. In the morning, she'd be a corpse, lying on the floor. Her roommates would be shocked at the sight of her, and the principal would call her mother and father. It would be another calamity for the family, as if Farid's illness wasn't enough. But she was doing this to save Farid for them, because the death of a girl was not like the death of a boy.

Her fingers were shaking, and ice flowed through her limbs. She needed water to swallow the pills. How could she swallow them dry? They'd stick in her throat. And if one went down, how would she swallow the second and the third and the tenth...? Where was the water? Wasn't there a jug in the room? A glass? Any liquid to wash her death down with? And buy back Farid?

She dragged herself to bed, burying her head under the quilt and trying, with stifled sobs, to muffle the sound of the papers that rustled whenever she turned her head. Her sobs were mixed with four thirsty words, "Water. I want water."

WHEN WIVES FALL ILL

Scene 1

A Waiting Room at a Clinic

Woman: Is the doctor in?

Nurse: Yes, ma'am, but he's busy at the moment.

Woman: I want to see him.

Nurse: Ahlan wa sahlan. But you'll have to wait a little while.

Woman: Wait? Why?

Nurse: Because the doctor sees the patients in turn.

Woman: Does he treat everyone like that?

Nurse: Like what, ma'am?

Woman: Do you expect me to wait like everyone else? No, forgive me, but there are appointments and then there's *la prestigieuse*.

Nurse: La prestigieuse?

Woman: Yes, *prestigieuse*. Haven't you heard this word before?

Nurse: No, no, I don't think so.

Woman: If you knew what it meant, you'd realize that someone like me can't wait!

Nurse: Why not, ma'am?

Woman: Why not, you ask? Don't you understand who people are, just by looking at them? Do you expect me to give a lecture about myself? Oh, oh, my chest feels tight. I'm ill… Yes, ill. I must be ill.

Nurse: Is there anything I can do for you?

Woman: Yes—you can get out of my sight. I'm starting to get annoyed with you.

Nurse: With me? Well, I'm sorry you don't like me. But you're going to have to wait at least half an hour.

Woman: Half an hour! No, no, that's impossible. Go and tell the doctor I'm not someone who waits at the door like those lot.

Nurse: It seems to me that ma'am's illness prevents her from doing anything—except talking. All right then, what are your symptoms? We need to tell the doctor *something*. Then he might let you in.

Woman: What are my symptoms? What an odd question! How would *I* know about my symptoms? I wouldn't be here if I knew! I canceled my appointment with the massage therapist and the hairdresser and—

Nurse: (Interrupting.) Well then, how did ma'am know she was sick?

Woman: Stop talking nonsense. I'm sick. I have to be sick with something—or some*things*. By the way, what are the illnesses that people can get?

Nurse: That people can get? I don't understand what you mean.

Woman: Don't you understand anything at all? It certainly doesn't look like it. I asked you what the doctor's clients usually complain of.

Nurse: (Gives a little laugh.) Oh, all sorts of things: diabetes, weak hearts, hardened arteries, nervous breakdowns…

Woman: What sort of silly diseases are those? I want a new disease. I want one that will cost me a lot of money—and be worth it. A disease that isn't common or vulgar. Everyone, even beggars, can have weak hearts or hardened arteries or colds. I want a rare disease with a Latin name.

Nurse: (Laughs.)

Woman: You think this is funny? Well, you can't be blamed—you don't know who I am. If you did, you wouldn't have let me wait here with…

(looks around) a man in a shirt with torn buttons and a woman who looks like a peasant or—at most—a maid. And you're still insisting on letting *them* in before *me*.

Nurse: That's because they booked their appointments before you did.

Woman: But I can, I can… By the way, I've been told the doctor charges outrageous fees.

Nurse: Outrageous? No, not always. Actually, he sometimes treats people for free.

Woman: (Jumps up in panic.) What? For free? No, no, that's terrible. For free? What do you take me for? I check myself into the hospital when I need to take a laxative! Listen… Now listen here, nurse, I don't want to be sick. I'll go back, go back… (The door opens and the doctor peers in.)

Doctor: Whose turn is it now?

Nurse: It's this gentleman's here. But this lady has been insisting that she needs to see you urgently because she's *unbearably* sick.

Doctor: Please come in. (Door closes.) Madam seems stressed.

Woman: Yes, I'm upset. Extremely upset.

Doctor: I'm sorry, perhaps I kept you waiting too long.

Woman: That, and other things.

Doctor: Please have a seat over here. I prefer to follow a process; it's better for me and for the patients.

Woman: Process? You're all murdering me with that word. What kind of process is this, one that puts maids before me? Perhaps you don't know me, Doctor.

Doctor: As a matter of fact, I know you well. I like to keep up with society news, you see, for a bit of light relief. I've seen pictures of you on more than one occasion.

Woman: (Relieved.) Oh, how nice. So you recognize me.

Doctor: How could I not? Aren't you a member of the Giraffe Club?

Woman: A member? I'm the President! I'm the President of the Giraffe Club, and a member of the Black and White Club, and of the water-skiing team.

Doctor: So Madam is a sportswoman.

Woman: Not exactly.

Doctor: What do you mean by "not exactly"?

Woman: I'm a modern woman, open to the idea of sports and so on—but I don't water ski. I just go to the parties.

Doctor: That's good. And how lucky for me—water-skiers don't tend to visit the doctor very often.

Woman: I hate that sport, it's so tiresome. But it is an aristocratic sport, as you know. And sometimes we have to do things we don't like for the sake of *le prestige*. (Sighs.) Life isn't always fun.

Doctor: Does Madam complain of anything?

Woman: That is just the question. I came here to ask you that question.

Doctor: Fine, the examination will tell us everything. But I was asking about any symptoms.

Woman: Oh, symptoms. What do you mean by symptoms?

Doctor: I mean, do you feel any pain? Is anything bothering you?

Woman: Yes, I'm bothered. You can't imagine how much your nurse bothered me.

Doctor: But she's a lovely nurse!

Woman: Lovely? She's rude… terribly rude!

Doctor: You must forgive her, Madam. She doesn't read society news. Let's go back to the question of diseases.

Woman: I don't know—just pick whatever disease you want for me.

Doctor: (Laughing.) Do you think this clinic has diseases for sale?

Woman: What do you care, as long as you're being paid? I need to bring several medicines home with me, and I want you to come and visit me once or twice.

Doctor: Just like that, for no reason? Is this some kind of ruse?

Woman: Not at all. I have to avoid going out in the evenings. And I need a good excuse to convince my friends that the reason I'm not going out is—

Doctor: —is that you're ill!

Woman: Yes.

Doctor: Am I to understand that Madam hates going out in the evenings?

Woman: Do I hate it? No. I show my face every night, for the sake of *le prestige*—I can't go to bed at ten o'clock like a chicken! But...

Doctor: But what?

Woman: There is a personal matter. It's forcing me not to go out in the evenings and to—

Doctor: —pretend to be ill?

Woman: Pretend? No, I truly am ill! And what I've seen from that wom— ohh, let's go back to what we were talking about.

Doctor: I'm a doctor, Madam. You can be frank with me. It might help me to identify your illness.

Woman: Don't you get it yet?

Doctor: Yes, I think I understand.

Woman: I need to be so sick that I can't go out in the evenings.

Doctor: And you're obliged to go out?

Woman: That's not the point—the thing is, I want to stop my husband from going out as well.

Doctor: By making him sick, too?

Woman: No, by making him feel it would be really low of him to go out and squander his money on gold-digging trollops while his wife is sick at home.

Doctor: Now I understand. He's squandering his money.

Woman: Please, Doctor, I don't care about the money. It's a matter of pride.

Doctor: Of course, since he's being pursued by this despicable woman.

Woman: She's despicable and a gold-digger, and… Doctor, you have no right to know my family secrets. I can't afford to waste time, I've already had to cancel my appointment with the massage therapist and the hairdresser. So please just tell me what disease I should come down with. But wait, is this a free clinic?

Doctor: Not completely free, no. It's free for people who deserve to be helped.

Woman: I was told you were a distinguished doctor, and that you've only recently returned from Europe. I didn't expect this "free" business.

Doctor: Don't worry, Madam, I'll charge you an amount you'll be happy with.

Woman: No, that's not what matters here. My friends will ask for the name of the doctor who treated me, and you know that le prestige makes us quite merciless. I'm a well-known woman. Well-known. Very well-known. I'm the president of the Giraffe Club and—

Doctor: —and a member of the water-skiing team and the Black and White Club and—

Woman: Good, so you know me. Then there's no need for me to tell you who I am.

Doctor: No need whatsoever. And I know that your husband goes out in the evenings, and that there's a woman who's trying to steal him away, and that you—

Woman: You're out of line, Doctor. That's not what I said.

Doctor: I was just trying to put my finger on your illness.

Woman: Are you making fun of me? Is that how you treat a woman of refinement? Forget it, I don't want to be sick. Open the door. I should have known better than to act so rashly as to seek out some small, unknown doctor who treats people's maids.

(She leaves, and the doctor's laughter follows her as she mutters: No manners, no manners whatsoever!)

Scene 2

The same woman at home. A friend of hers comes in.

Woman: Oh, it's you. I thought you might stop by.

Friend: Of course! We missed you so much.

Woman: I'm sick, as you can see.

Friend: Sick? It doesn't show on your face at all.

Woman: Don't you believe me? Look—five bottles of medicine. Oh my God, I'm suffocating. (Calling the maid.) Latifa! Latifa! Open the window. I need some fresh air.

Friend: Poor thing, you missed the party yesterday. We didn't know you were sick.

Woman: Why would I have stayed at home, if I hadn't been sick? I never miss anything.

Friend: (Gives a sly laugh.) D'ya want the truth? It had crossed our minds that there was another reason.

Woman: (Nervously.) Another reason? Whatever do you mean?

Friend: You know very well what I mean.

Woman: Do you mean that woman?

Friend: Yes.

Woman: Why would someone like me pay any attention to someone like her? A foolish, reckless woman.

Friend: But she's a clever hunter!

Woman: I don't care about her. I didn't even stop my husband from going to yesterday's party.

Friend: And would he have obeyed you, if you'd tried?

Woman: Ha! Don't forget that I have the upper hand in this house.

Friend: But your husband is like a spoiled child.

Woman: That's if I lavish my money on him. I know how to punish him when I want to.

Friend: Talk about those two is starting to go around.

Woman: It's not his fault. She's after his money. It's her. She's the one who's chasing him, but he's faithful. Very faithful.

Friend: That's not what people are saying.

Woman: People? What people? A bunch of foolish, penniless gossips? I could destroy that woman in twenty-four hours if I wanted to.

Friend: And why haven't you wanted to?

Woman: I'm sick! I don't have time to deal with her foolishness. I'm sick, don't you understand?

Friend: I understand, I do. But I don't like hearing people say you've stopped going to parties because you're dying of jealousy. You know how people love to wag their tongues.

Woman: Me, die of jealousy? And for whom? A boneless, watery meal of a woman? A cheap, gold-digging, penniless widow? I wonder how a woman like that can be welcomed into society with open arms. Who is she to deserve to be a member of the Giraffe Club, and the Black and White Club—

Friend: —and a member of the Horse-Riding Club and the Friends of Dutch Cows Club, plus she's a friend of all the embassies and the diplomatic missions, too. She's a success. A big success.

Woman: (Calls the maid.) Latifa, come here, come and open the other window and hand me that box of cigarettes. I need to smoke, even though my illness doesn't permit it. (Lights a cigarette.)

Friend: You're very stressed, my dear.

Woman: No, I'm ill. There's a difference between being stressed and being ill. You're getting on my nerves today.

Friend: I'm sorry. I thought I was keeping you amused with all this talk.

Woman: Yes, you're amusing me—amusement is all this calls for, really, but it's at my expense. Listen, I don't want—I can't bear—to hear anyone mention my name in the same breath as that bitch.

Friend: It's not your name that people connect her with, it's your husband's!

Woman: Openly, just like that?

Friend: Openly, just like that. He dances with her and drinks with her, and people say they were seen together at the market and in the casino at one of the hotels up in the mountains. And they say he paid fifty lira at a party last week to buy her a rose to pin to her dress.

Woman: That dog!

Friend: And people's tongues don't need any encouragement, my dear.

Woman: But—

Friend: But what? They're always looking for a story, any story to prattle on about, and your husband—if you allow me—is lacking in the art of discretion.

Woman: Would they forgive him, then, if he knew how to hide his relationship with her?

Friend: So you admit there's a relationship.

Woman: Me? Not at all. I'm just commenting on what you said. My husband can't have had bad intentions. He is open-minded and easy-going, that's all, just easy-going. My God, people always think the worst.

Friend: Don't get angry, darling. Your nerves are shot.

Woman: And I'm ill, too.

Friend: But you shouldn't stay in bed all day. That'll make you feel even worse.

Woman: I know, but it's the doctor's orders.

Friend: Forget about the doctors. They make a big deal of everything. You must come to the party at the Shooting Club tonight.

Woman: No, I won't go out. I'll stay in bed, with my husband right beside me!

Friend: I can tell you for sure that, if you go out, he'll stick by your side. At least for a few days.

Woman: What do you mean?

Friend: That other woman isn't a threat anymore. She's found fresh prey.

Woman: (Curious.) Fresh prey?

Friend: Yes, and it's a fat one this time. Very fat. Remember that man who was living abroad, the one who came back from Argentina a month ago?

Woman: Yes, yes.

Friend: He's handing out money like there's no tomorrow, and people can't stop talking about all the farms and stables and mansions he owns over there.

Woman: Which—

Friend: That damn woman has managed to snare him good and tight.

Woman: So—

Friend: Yes! It's over. Your husband's been alone for the past three nights, drinking at the bar and talking politics.

Woman: And what about her?

Friend: There's been no sign of her. People say he invited her to Argentina.

Woman: This town will breathe a lot freer if she accepts that invitation.

Friend: Yes. The gang have been betting you'll show up tonight with your husband.

Woman: And were you one of the betters?

Friend: I'll be honest with you and say yes.

Woman: In that case, I'll help you win your bet. (Calls the maid.) Latifa! Latifa, get my bath ready for me. (To her friend:) I mustn't give in to illness. A hot bath will be really good for me. Life's too short for us to waste it in bed—isn't that so, my dear?

SALT

Her mistress's voice quavered in its bluish tone as she called out, "Clear the table!" The dishes were still full and untouched, and the master of the house pushed his chair back, grumbling.

She flicked her anxious gaze between the table and her mistress's eyes. At first, she thought the couple had fought. Maybe the husband had gotten up in a huff, and the wife had stopped eating before she had even started. But the woman shouted at her, "Take it! Clear it away! Do you call this food? No... taste it first! Let's see if you can stand food that's been cooked with sea water." And she paired her demand with an action: picking up a spoon, the mistress scooped some peas into it and shoved it into her mouth. As soon as it touched the tip of her tongue, she felt her insides lurch and her eyes began to water. Covering her mouth with her palm, she ran to the kitchen to rid herself of its contents and wash out the saltiness at the nearest tap.

She muttered to herself as she wiped her face. Yes, it tasted like it had been cooked in sea water, but she didn't remember putting more than a single sprinkle of salt in the pot. It had been an ordinary amount, the same as she always used, and her hand was as precise as any scale, never wrong and never betrayed by the ingredients it measured out. So, what had happened to turn her food into "bitter apple and sea water," as her mistress had called it? Had she salted it twice by mistake, and ruined it? But even if she had absentmindedly done it twice, the taste would still have been bearable. So how had it happened, when she herself had learned at the hands of Wahiba, the house's cook since forever and a master of the craft, one who could turn dirt into a delicious dish if she liked? Whenever she had some free time, she used to hover around Wahiba, watching or helping her, and Wahiba had been content to let her do it, saying, "You know, if one day my hands fail me, no one but you will take over from old Wahiba and carry on her art."

It was as if Wahiba had known exactly what things would come to after her hands were stricken by the tremors, and she became a relic, kept on only to honor a promise. Wahiba had never known a house other than this one. She had started working for the family before her master was born, and after him, four siblings had followed. They had grown up, married and moved out, while she stayed on in the house, queen of its kitchen, tickling her employers' taste buds and gaining their favor with all her concoctions, until she was betrayed by her weakening eyes and trembling hands. After that, she withdrew into a corner from which she could manage all the action: counting the pots, refusing to let meddling hands change anything, and overseeing this girl—she would accept no one else as her next-in-line. She had been the girl's ticket into the house, and with that as leverage, the girl would never chafe at Wahiba's instructions or the things she insisted on, or the comparisons she made between them.

She stood there, wondering how the meal had been ruined, looking around in all directions and trying to come up with an explanation. She remembered taking one spoonful from this specific container. Yes, one—and she remembered thinking it was too much, and not pouring it all in. But who would believe her? Even though he rarely shouted, her master's voice now reached her ears, sharp and decisive, "Get rid of her and find yourself someone else!"

"This just reminds us what a gem Wahiba is," her mistress added, "Not even ten people could fill Wahiba's shoes! Twenty years she cooked for this house, and she never spoiled anything, not once."

No Sir, not ten, nor twenty, nor even fifty people could fill my shoes. Say it again, Sir, so I can hear you. Say it to steady my trembling hands. Say it and let all of them hear you—I don't want anything more.

Wahiba truly wanted no more than that. From where she sat, in the small room off the kitchen, she broke into a smile that widened until it turned into silent laughter, as she remembered how she had waited until Hamida wasn't looking and slipped a fistful of salt into the pot.

NIGHT OF RIDDANCE

"Mama, how are we going to get rid of Shadow?"
"We'll put him in a big sack."
"Which sack?"
"One of the empty sugar sacks. A big one, big enough for Shadow and…"
"And what?"
"Nothing. Eat up."
"And then what?"
"And then the grocer will take him somewhere far away from here."
"Will he walk there?"
"He'll walk, or maybe take the tram."
"Won't Shadow find his way back, Mama?"
"That mangy old thing? No. And if he does, he'll have no choice but to drown in the sea."
"And a big fish would eat him, right?"
"The ifrits can eat him for all I care. It's either me or that blind old thing in this house."

This was a conversation Umm Saad had heard more than once, a story the mother told her little one every time they sat down at the table, to encourage him to eat. The discussion between mother and son wasn't new, but this time Umm Saad felt it wasn't a joke. She'd just gotten home after visiting a neighbor when she was met on the stairs by a pair of round black eyes peering out from a pleasant, chubby face.

"If you're so smart, then guess where Shadow is?"

Her grandson was about to jump in and answer his own challenge, but at just that moment, his mother looked out from the top of the stairs and shrieked at him so loudly that he stumbled and would have tripped, if his grandmother's hands hadn't quickly caught him. Holding the little one's hand, she lifted a heavy leg to climb the stairs to her room. She threw her black shawl onto the bed and rushed to the back balcony, where Shadow usually sat. But all she found was a zinc dish with its chipped paint and a leftover bone that had been too hard for the dog's teeth.

He wasn't there. And that's when she remembered the story.

She stood frozen, looking at the bone. It was clean and white—Shadow hadn't left a scrap on it, as if he'd sensed it would be his last meal in this house and that, after this bone, the elderly dog's fate hung in the grip of two spiteful lips.

Her heart sensed this was the scene of a new tragedy, one of many minor tragedies that would hardly deserve the name, if their source hadn't been her daughter-in-law—her daughter-in-law and an old dog. In her daughter-in-law's eyes, they were equally matched, so she could condemn the old dog to a fate where he ended up as fish food or was abandoned in a vacant lot. And who could say it wouldn't be Umm Saad's turn, after the dog?

That foul woman wanted "a sack big enough for Shadow and…" She would stop mid-sentence each time she said it, as though, while gleefully describing her plans, she was actually imagining her mother-in-law stuffed into the sack and carried away somewhere—anywhere—by a hired boy.

What would Sami say if he knew?

Yes, Sami. The other, older one saw nothing in the dog's fate beyond the normal ending deserved by an aging dog. Perhaps he would give a callous smile if he heard his wife saying "a sack big enough for Shadow and…" Yes, what would Sami say?

His image popped into her mind. A strong young man climbing the ship's stairs with the enthusiasm of someone who's throwing himself into the arms of the unknown. When he'd reached the top of the stairs, he pushed back a lock of hair that hung over his forehead, waved at his mother, and shouted with his powerful voice, "Don't cry, Ummi. Take care of Shadow for me. I want him pampered, the way I'd pamper him myself if I was there. And don't forget to bathe him, or else he'll be eaten up by ticks."

His laughter tumbled down on her from above until it was swept away by a long blast of the ship's horn. When they got home from the port, Shadow met her at the top of the stairs. He fawned over her, rubbing his nose against her shoe as if he sensed that, now that Sami was gone, affection would come only from her. She hadn't been particularly welcoming to him before—she'd hit him once or twice when, as a puppy, he'd chewed and frayed the corner of the bedspread. She'd often argued with Sami over whether the dog was of any use, and she'd been the first to stand up to him when he jokingly suggested bringing home a female dog to make a family of black puppies. But now that Sami had left home, she was prepared to forget all that, and to love Shadow as she'd never loved him before. She was true to her word: Shadow's breakfast bread was now softer, and his milk bowl unaccustomedly filled to the brim. And when it was time for his bath, she didn't hold back with the soap. She washed him, groomed his long black hair with a wooden comb, and kissed him—she, who had long warned Sami that it was foolish to kiss dogs because their breath was poisonous, and sprayed out germs she couldn't name.

When Sami's first letter arrived, she picked up the red-and-blue-edged envelope and told the dog, "Sami says hello! He's in med school now, and you might not recognize him when he comes home to us wearing glasses. All doctors wear glasses. Prepare yourself to move into his clinic and become a distinguished dog, the doctor's dog—Doctor Sami." But she was too embarrassed to say out loud, "And I'll be the doctor's mother." She was so happy she cut him a slice of the cake her daughter-in-law had made and snuck it to him, first biting off the edges decorated with raisins and grated coconut. After that, they became friends.

A dog's friendship makes up for so much. A person can't help but complain about her daughter-in-law. But if her son takes his wife's side, and the maid doesn't care, then who else was left for her but Shadow?

He was the only one she could open her heart to, and she'd pour her complaints into his long ears.

"Shadow, have you ever seen anyone as foolish as my daughter-in-law? She boils the potatoes before she fries them. She's jealous of me and isn't ashamed to tell me that getting made up is 'not for old women.' She won't let me talk to her friends and even turns up her nose at sharing a table with me. As if she's giving me charity by letting me live in my own son's home! Any woman who marries off a son is crazy. I'll hate you if you get married, Shadow. I'll hate you."

And on many nights, when the daughter-in-law would close the door on herself and her husband, and the old woman was left alone in the living room, she'd go about darning her son's socks and talking to Shadow about Sami's news, and how the university had exempted him from tuition because he was hardworking, and how he was the very cleverest of all the students. She'd say that, and then she'd get up to take a bundle of letters from the cubbyhole so she could laboriously revisit every line. Shadow would know these were from his absent master, and he'd wag his tail in delight, only growing despondent when he saw the old woman wipe away a tear that was fogging up her glasses.

This mutual affection between the two elderly creatures was a great irritation to the daughter-in-law. It irked her to see her mother-in-law find comfort in that animal's company, so she made their relationship the butt of jokes and mockery that allowed her to say, within her mother-in-law's earshot, "Animals become senile, too…"

At this, her husband would laugh stupidly, as if she meant a neighbor, not his mother.

It didn't stop at jokes. She was always ready to channel her emotions into hostilities, which she expressed with her feet as she kicked the dog, not caring about his sad howling, when he crept up to the dining table, or licked the little one's legs, or barked at one of her friends.

She kept saying that she wasn't prepared to put up with two senile creatures in the house. And she'd meant it—Shadow was gone now, poor thing! What kind of ending was this, to crown his kindly old age, to reward months and years of loyalty?

A sack big enough for Shadow and…

Would her turn come at the hands of this vicious woman?

The old woman stayed frozen on the balcony. Never before had loneliness swelled in her heart as it did now.

She cried until her tears were spent.

And when night fell, she roused herself.

She had to do something for Shadow, for the sake of their old age spent together.

She struggled down the stairs on feet that had a hard time doing as they were told. She couldn't find the grocer's boy, to ask where he'd taken Shadow, and she got nowhere when she took her strange question to others. "Did anyone see Shadow being carried away in a sack?"

They'd listen and shrug. They didn't understand what it would mean to her—Shadow's death, and her own death to follow at the hand of his executioner. That poor thing! Nine loyal years hadn't earned him the right to die at home.

She made her way westward toward the sea, taking the road that went downhill to the lighthouse, then turning left, pushed along effortlessly by the wind. It was a black moonless night, the streetlights blind and unlit, and not a sound to be heard except for the senseless pounding of the waves against the rocks that stood along the ancient shoreline.

Her eyes strained to cut through the gloom, trying to make out Shadow in his sack, or maybe on his feet, looking at her from between the rocks, or being carried by a gentle wave that refused to claim corpses. But all she could see was darkness and the reflection of distant lights on the water. She set off walking again, following the long Corniche, which led her to the suburbs, not stopping unless she heard barks.

She only realized she had strayed far away when she slumped onto a rock to rest, delivering her wounded reproach to the night. But the night didn't answer. It remained silent, and its silence was broken only by the distant barking of stray dogs, and not a one of them was Shadow.

OUT OF TIME

THE MAD BELL-RINGER

Sunday woke in our village to the sound of cheerful and lively silver chimes and, before shielding hands had been lifted to foreheads, eyes had already met with questioning looks: if that was the church bell, then the bell-ringer was definitely not Abu Masoud. And when we hurried to the church square to investigate, we saw all the vigor of a twenty-year-old being blown into a bell, the chimes of which had lost their even tones when Abu Masoud reached his sixties.

So then, Father Yacoub had done it—he'd shown us proof that, if he wanted something, he would get it done. He hadn't acted out of stubbornness or prejudice, but rather because he was sorry to hear the bell's call being smothered by those feeble chimes that all of us had noticed. All of us, that is, except Abu Masoud, who seemed to have lost his sense of pitch with the onset of the tremors in his hands. He was coming apart, breaking down, confusing things. You'd find him ringing morning bells in the evening, and some people claimed that one man, on the day he was to be married in church, begged Abu Masoud to pay attention and not ring funeral bells for the wedding.

Having grown somewhat deaf, the man couldn't be blamed for failing to notice the incoherence of his tunes. It was as if he had been born hanging on to that rope: he pulled it in the morning so the sleeping village would shake itself free of the night, and he pulled it in the evening to announce the end of the day. In our village, Abu Masoud and the bell were one and the same thing, a single being that continued, for forty long years, to mark the occasions of our births and our weddings. Not once had Abu Masoud been late or lax or been kept away from his duties by absence, illness, or indisposition.

The tremors that begin in a person's sixties had never crossed his mind, nor ours, and continuity was a well-established rule in our tradition. But Father Yacoub, while his beard was still black, had wanted to bring a little youth to the church, and he had started with the bell and bell-ringer. As soon as he had finished giving his first mass in church, he had called Abu Masoud and asked him how long he had been in his job. Abu Masoud had given him a smile that spread as wide as his toothless mouth could stretch, saying, "Forty... forty years, Father."

The very last thing he had expected was for the priest to say, "Don't you think it's time for you to rest now?"

In our village, we weren't used to things being decided this quickly, except on that Sunday morning when we hurried to church—just like Abu Masoud—driven by those cheerful and lively silver chimes. And when the man saw someone else hanging onto the bell rope, his eyes went red and his mustache flared, and he would have strangled the boy with his bare hands, if it weren't for a group of people who surrounded him and begged him, in the name of the church's sanctity, not to lose his temper while prayers were being held. After the service, the pastor sought him out and explained frankly that his arms had become too weak to pull a rope, or ring such a bell, the chimes of which were meant to echo in the valleys all around.

From that Sunday on, Abu Masoud's only concern was to knock on our doors to stir us up against the priest, and to make fun of the boy who had turned the bell into a toy. He cast solemn oaths in our faces, vowing never to set foot in the church while it was led by a pastor like this one. He would spread his dry palm out for everyone to see, saying, "Look at how the rope has eaten away a layer of my hand—and that one wants to teach me how to ring a bell!"

Then he would angrily close his fist and send a hearty curse to hang on the pastor's beard. We would listen to him and laugh, then try to comfort him, or we'd start teasing him by saying, "And when you die, who else do you have but him to ring the bell for you?"

And he would go back to ranting and raving, saying, "I'd rather die a blighted infidel than have that priest lead my funeral service or have the bell rung for me by that..."

Once, he disappeared from the village for days, and rumors flourished. They said he had died of vexation, and that he had abandoned the village forever, and that he had done this and done that... One of the things we heard was that he had gone to the neighboring villages, looking to become a bell-ringer for their churches, but when he came back, we realized that his hopes had been dashed at every bell he had approached. In any case, he had stopped standing in front of the church bell and would stand instead at the threshold of the belfry door, holding his arms in the air like someone who was pulling a rope and making ringing noises with his voice: Ding-dong... ding-dong. And then one night, the village woke in a panic to the sound of the church bell ringing in unsteady tones that shattered the absolute silence of the night. The villagers found the man hanging from the rope, his hair and mustache flaring. He was hurtling down with it, then almost flying into the air as it jerked back up with the swing of the bell. His fingers had stiffened around the rope and his nails dug into its fibers.

That day, a new person, with a new name, was introduced to the village. It was as if, before this, he had lived without a name. And now who knows Abu Masoud by any name other than "The Mad Bell-Ringer"?

OUT OF TIME

EVERYTHING WAS SILENCED

The music howled, and dreadful screams fell like sharp knives onto the broad canopies that stretched out from the tops of the parasol pines. It felt as if the trees were rejecting the music. They shook their branches in a determined refusal that could never have been mistaken for swaying in time with that rabid howling. The howls had been blaring out from the café since noon that day—and since every noon, of every day, since that shameless idiot had opened his café, and this beautiful place overlooking the valley had been condemned to being an attraction for those young men and women. A person couldn't tell one from the other because all of them, men and women alike, wore tight pants and colorful shirts, and had lanky hair hanging in clumps over their foreheads.

Was this what today's generation had come to? Abu Makhoul spat for the tenth or eleventh time, gripping the armrests of the ancient chair as he looked around at the abandoned items: faded chairs, tables where no two legs were the same length, and that kindly old couch. Umm Makhoul had covered it with an embroidered sheet, shielding it from the daylight sun with a curtain that was strung between two trees, and, if any of the café's customers wanted a siesta, he would find fresh bedding on the couch, however humble it may have looked. And if Abu Makhoul fell asleep, he didn't have to worry about someone surprising him, because Umm Makhoul was there. She ran the café through the little hatch in the kiosk, the shelves of which she stocked with rows of large and small bottles of arak, and a bowl or two of a mix of roasted chickpeas, peanuts, and watermelon seeds.

And that was all they offered to whoever wanted an honest drink and paid for it with honest money. Umm Makhoul felt she was at least three quarters of the café, since it stood on a plot of land that she had inherited, and its trees were pines that had grown there since long before the people who had passed down the land, and their heirs, had been born. As for how it became a café, that was simple: a roof made from a few straw mats, spread out over logs that were nailed between the trees; some tables and chairs; the kiosk at one end; Umm Makhoul inside the kiosk; and him out here by himself. He willingly served up the orders, giving some people theirs on the house, because he would never take money if the customer was a friend. After all, there was still some good to be found in the world. And when the customers came, they felt as if they were at home, enjoying their evening drink amidst the scent of the pines and looking out over the deep, majestic valley, where only the sounds of cicadas could be heard. If one of them grew tipsy after having a drink or two, he might earn himself a scolding and a battle of words with Abu Makhoul, the son of a wandering poet whose verses were part of the village's weddings and funerals.

Every summer, and for more than twenty years, his café would attract those who loved the peace and quiet. He would open it with the first signs of summer and close it at the end of October, when biting cold winds became a feature of the fall weather. He didn't actually "close" the café. All he had to do was stack the tables and chairs in a corner and gather up the straw mats so the season's rains wouldn't wear them out. Then he and Umm Makhoul would go down to their little house, which stood on one of the valley's strong shoulders.

And then a year ago, this new café opened. Abu Makhoul didn't call it a café, he called it a filthy name, which he felt it thoroughly deserved. At first, he wasn't too bothered when it opened right next to his place. Each would earn the livelihood God had assigned to him, and he had a small set of customers and knew every one of them. Their number hardly grew or shrunk; they came to his café every night, and most were locals from the village, not summer holidaymakers, who tended to look for somewhere more modern and sophisticated. Only one of the holidaymakers used to come to his shop every day to smoke a narghile, and he only stopped visiting when this scourge had opened up. It was started by a Frenchified Beiruti who aimed to draw in a younger crowd. The tools of his trade were garishly colored chairs which looked—to quote Umm Makhoul—like a whore's face, and that box which kept on howling, record after record. The bodies would sway, gently at first, then harder, and then the dancers would be possessed by ifrits and taken over by hysteria, and they would whirl like dervishes in a trance. And the box would bellow and bellow, and howl and howl, and then the noise would dim and soften and fade away, only to come back again, suddenly, with raving bellows or rabid howls. The customers would pour in, their bodies crowding in closer and their faces contorting into ugly grimaces. There was not a man's face nor a woman's among them—they were just faces with wild eyes, blurred features, and fake identities.

He was used to men being men and women being pure and demure, either mothers or young women whose eyelashes dripped with modesty and who, if they drank, would do so shyly, taking only a tiny sip, like a bird's, from the edge of their husband's glass. As for those others, they held their sinful yellow drinks in full view, the foam bubbling and spilling over onto their twisted necks and scrawny, emaciated, sun-crisped bodies.

And then all of a sudden, his customers disappeared. They fled from the deluge of voices and noise. His café no longer attracted anyone except a passer-by who wanted a drink of water from the cool earthenware jug that leaned against a stone.

Today in particular, the box was twice as crazy, as if it had been possessed by a thousand ifrits at once. It hadn't stopped since nine in the morning, and it played a single tune that never changed. And those troops of young people came running, afraid of missing out on the shoddy merriment, the noise of which drowned out every other thing: the peals of the church bell, which, on Sundays, used to echo in the valleys; the non-stop chirping of the cicadas; the honking of car horns. And Abu Makhoul sat alone at the table. Umm Makhoul had left him and gone to visit her brother, so he surrendered his white head to his helpless palms. The summer, or at least most of it, had gone by, and he hadn't been able to cover the cost of what he'd paid for supplies. He didn't know what he would do when winter hit. The other place was boiling over with people, it snatched up their bodies and never threw them back. They piled in, flesh against flesh, and its walls swelled up to make room for more. And the only person in his café was him.

"Why don't you buy a 'box,' Abu Makhoul?" some people asked.

He swallowed a curse that was about to leap to his lips. Buy a box? And turn his café into… into… And then he went quiet. They understood what he meant, and there was no need to sully his lips with all that vulgarity. He would rather die than kill off his manhood, or allow it to be said that Abu Makhoul had opened a—

He couldn't bring himself to say it, even to himself.

Pain pounded like falling hammers onto the white head as it leaned on palms that groped in vain for a long-lost peace of mind. And the sound of that rabid music filled the air, closing in on all sides and suffocating him. It built a wall in front of him, so he could barely see either the sun slipping down behind the valley, or the hills being cloaked in majestic darkness, to which the houses on the mountain surrendered in calm tranquility. He had been stuck to his chair since that morning and didn't remember having eaten, or craving food, or feeling hungry. Every one of his organs cried out under a barrage of needle-like pricks. And that fiendish buzzing rose up in his head, multiplied, and grew stronger. He thought of catching up with his wife, but felt his legs were too weak to carry him. The hours of the evening passed, one after the other, and Umm Makhoul didn't come home. Perhaps she had accepted her family's invitation to spend the night and had found some peace of mind that she hadn't known since the beginning of summer. The lights wilted in the houses that dotted the mountain slopes, and the night seemed mightier and more wondrous. Nothing encroached on its majesty now except those piercing screams. The contraption was spinning; the bodies were spinning; the earth was spinning; and Abu Makhoul's head was spinning. Finally, the café spat out exhausted patron after exhausted patron. The last customer left, and the owner carried on settling accounts with the waiter without bothering to shut off the hellish noise. And then everything was silenced. And the quiet was all the more powerful because it came after every sound had been stilled.

   In the morning, the noise didn't start up again. And the puppets who came to the café turned back on their heels. Two surprising things had happened in one night. The café owner had returned in the morning to blast his noise into the village sky, only to find the box in scattered ruins. And he'd found a big rock that was as good as proof of the deliberate act. He didn't need to rack his brains. Who else could it be but Abu Makhoul who, along with his wife, had never hidden their distress at this sudden new fever, and who hadn't been ashamed to fling curses, like vengeful rockets, at his face? All the evidence pointed to his elderly head. Did envy really push people this far? The man began to bellow, and his shouts reached the villagers' ears. Everyone heard them except Abu Makhoul. He was found lying face-down on a table, a large empty liquor bottle in his hand, his fingers stiffened around its neck.

THE RIVAL

This was the eighth hotel building she had circled that day, trying to find a door that didn't reveal so much luxury that it made her feel as if someone like her couldn't possibly intrude on all that to ask for work.

"I'm a washerwoman, Sir. I can work all day without getting tired and…"

The department manager cut her off, hardly bothering to process what she was saying. "No, no, we don't want your services. We use electricity for our washing."

Electricity, electricity… She moved on, taking her quest to another hotel and circling it for an hour or more before finding a back door she could use to step inside and ask her question—only to hear the same answer. But she didn't give up. She couldn't go home until she'd found a job that would quell her husband's rage and calm his resentment, so he wouldn't beat her again like he'd done the night before. He'd proven no different from Saada's, Ayousha's, and Umm Hassan's husbands, and had stolen her feelings of superiority from back when, as they sat chatting together, they would say, "Wahiba is the only one whose husband is like the city men and never beats his wife."

It was true that her husband hadn't used to humiliate her. The situation must have reached a crisis point for him, to have made him lose his temper and hit her on the mouth with the back of his hand, just because, when he asked her to pass him the water jug, she'd been fanning the fire that burned in their yard and hadn't heard him. He had called her twice and she still hadn't heard. After he hit her, she had raised her voice as high as it went and screamed at him that he should be ashamed of himself, but he'd immediately given her a punch to the cheek and another to her chest, then pushed her so hard that she fell to the ground.

Wahiba had never claimed that her husband was a pleasant man. He had a harsh nature that never left him, except when the moment came for him to get his hands on his wages or on Wahiba's pay from a washing job: only then would he break into a smile that disappeared under his drooping mustache, choking out a prayer for Wahiba to be granted good health and strong arms.

She could tell that, even though he was sometimes kind to her, he didn't love her, and she had never harbored any hopes that he would fall madly in love with her. She hadn't forgotten the time her mother had leaned in close, trying to make Wahiba seem more attractive, doing her best to blind him to her large mouth and coarse, horse-tail hair, saying, "She's got an arm on her that never gets tired. She can work for hire in the fields and carry water from the well."

He had scratched his head and twisted his mustache, and then tried to smile as he mumbled, "Okay, fine."

And on their wedding night, he said, "Listen, Wahiba, we don't belong here, where we're just hired hands, taking meals as payment for our service and barely making ends meet. Our place is there, in the city, where my cousin and all my uncles went. They came back with silver in their purses, and they used it to buy land.

"We'll stay there ten, twenty years. Then we'll come home and buy a small plot of land. Listen, we'll even build ourselves a room of stone."

She had started in surprise as she heard him, for the first time ever, laugh out loud.

Ever since they had consummated their marriage, she had lived in the city with him and had never once visited her village. She missed her family and friends, but he wouldn't let her go back, not even for her sister's wedding or her mother's funeral. News reached her that the villagers were accusing her of being ungrateful and had called her vile names she didn't deserve. But her husband scolded her every time she begged for a visit home. "Wallah, I won't go back there until I'm either a landowner or carried in a coffin!"

Yes, he had only married her because she was as strong as a horse and had never once hesitated to take on a washing job. Lira by lira, her pay went into his pocket. From it, all he spent was the price of some coarse, dark loaves, a few olives, and oil for the lamp. Day after day, he'd count his savings and say, "A feddan costs such-and-such liras. We've got a long road ahead of us, and our land is priced like gold."

She was overcome with rapturous joy on those occasions when she felt, as she handed him a lira, that he valued her, and that she counted for something in his ambitions. And when he talked to her about the land—sometimes calling it "our land that we're going to buy"—and patted her on the shoulder, it made her happy.

The turning point had come more than a year ago, when she heard about something quite peculiar. One of her oldest customers asked her not to come in anymore for the weekly wash because now they had a new washer—an electric one.

She knew many other washerwomen: Mabrouka, Khadra, Fattoum. As for "Electric," she didn't recognize her among the competition.

When she asked her customer to explain, and the woman realized she'd misunderstood, she laughed from the bottom of her heart. "You idiot, I didn't mean another woman. It's a machine that washes and wrings out the laundry better than you or any genie of a washerwoman can."

She spent that entire evening thinking about what she'd heard from the woman. Keeping this strange news to herself bothered her, so she told her husband. He spent a long time thinking and then said, "Wallah, I've never heard anyone else speak of such a thing. Perhaps it's a trick the woman used to get rid of you."

She challenged his suspicions, reeling off that she was the best at scraping dirt out of shirt gussets and collars, and the best at pegging clothes on the line, so they hung crisp and fresh, like new sheets of paper.

The next day, she hurried back to the woman and begged to see how the machine did the washing. Proudly, the woman began to demonstrate, not noticing how Wahiba's eyes popped as she watched the drum churning with soap and water in the white container, and the clothes coming out of it all floaty and clean. Wahiba went home thinking about her white enemy and sat, lost in thought, at the edge of the mat. Her husband asked her what was wrong, and she told him about the washing machine. "That woman is the first bead in the rosary," he said. "Her neighbors will be next, then all the neighborhood women, and then every woman in the city will follow."

And her husband was right. A few days later, another of her customers told her, with no hint of sympathy, not to come back. In the same week, she heard it from a third client, and, in less than a month, she had heard it from five homes. Within a year, doing the washing by hand had become old-fashioned.

What hurt Wahiba most was that the women whose laundry she had faithfully washed for so many years hadn't spared a thought for how they'd cut off her livelihood, and how their machines had deprived her of her daily bread. It tormented her even more to see how her husband resented her unemployment; night after night, he wore a constant frown and refused to speak to her until, when she kept coming home empty-handed, he blew up at her, screaming, "Do you think I married you for your soft hands? Who would've even looked at a woman like you if it wasn't for a hardworking man like me?" Then he accused her of being stupid because those women had chosen a machine over her.

How she hated that machine! One day, she walked past a store and saw several of them lined up, one beside the other. There were ten or more in the store window. She imagined they were sneering at her, mocking her wrinkled hands and the scarf pulled tight around her head. She wanted to do something, maybe smash them to pieces, or jam their gears so they wouldn't work. The blood rushed to her face, and she stayed there for a long time until the store assistant noticed and came up to her to ask, with a condescending snark, "What does Madame want?" At this, she left, insults quivering on her lips.

That night, her husband had beaten her, and she felt incapable of being useful.

She felt even more useless in the morning, when she tried her hand as a housemaid. The lady of the house had sent her away after two hours, telling her she was an ignorant slob who didn't know how to make a bed: she had piled up the pillows willy-nilly, and left the sheet-ends dangling in a clumsy mess.

She had never been anything but a washerwoman, and she could never be anything else.

Wahiba kept circling the eighth hotel. She was unsure how to get in and afraid—if she did get in—of hearing the same dreaded words. She tried to slip in through one door, but a hotel maid stopped her and sent her away. Then she came in through a different entrance and immediately saw a group of gentlemen who were sunk deep in comfortable seats, gazing thoughtfully at the thick clouds of smoke that hung in the air.

She nearly tripped as she turned to make her escape.

Finally finding a back door that led to the kitchen, so she approached the cook and said, "Listen, Uncle, I'm a washerwoman—"

He cut her off, pushing her aside with a wooden spoon and telling her it was none of his business whether or not she was a washerwoman.

She didn't know how many doors she tried after that, and how many corridors she trudged through before a porter took pity on her and led her to the man in charge.

She stood for a second, hesitantly watching his face, because she sensed he was about to say, "electric washing machine."

The first words trembled on her lips, "Listen, Sir, I— I'm—"

"You're what?"

She went quiet, as if afraid to finish her sentence.

The man was irritated and yelled, "Speak up, woman! What is it?"

"Look, Sir, I'm a washerwoman. I can wash by hand and I can use electricity to do the washing—yes, I can use electricity if you want! Just let me do the job, and don't pay me if you don't like my work."

How the idea came to her in that split second, she had no clue. She said it and closed her eyes, replaying in her mind how her old customer had poured hot water and a white powder into the machine, then turned it on, making it whirl the wad of clothes around with soap and water in its drum.

It wasn't hard, and she'd been wrong to think so. She'd get the hang of it for sure, if she saw how it worked once or twice.

She'd give it a try—didn't she have eyes and hands and a brain like the other women who'd learned to use the machine to do their washing?

Her limbs trembled as she thought about the risk she was taking, but she didn't want to back down. Her eyes remained eagerly fixed on the man's face.

Perhaps she didn't hear him tell the porter to "take her to the laundry room and ask Zakiyya to find work for her to do," because she was still saying, over and over, that she was a washerwoman who could do the washing with her own two hands—or with electricity!

OUT OF TIME

THE ROC FLEW OVER SHAHRABAN

Slowly, we raised our heads as hellish cries echoed in our ears, and we looked up in awe and fear. The sky was a summery blue with no trace of a cloud, and the sun had spread out, occupying every corner. We lowered our gazes, licking our bluish lips as we exchanged panicked glances. Our cracked feet were rooted to the furrowed mud, as if our slightest movement might stir up the screeching. We chewed over our terror for a few minutes, our parted lips emitting silence. Our mounts were as terrified as we were, and they scattered around the courtyard at the inn, fear spurring them to shake off the torpor of the midday heat.

The men began to pour in, forgetting to hold up the muddy hems of their robes as they edged into the courtyard. They gathered in silence, stealing furtive looks at each other, waiting for one among them to muster the courage to find his voice.

Finally, Abbas cleared his throat. His voice seemed huge in the blistering stillness.

"Why have you suddenly lost your tongues? He said it before he died, and he said it while he was dying, and he died with the same words on his lips: 'It was bigger than a roc bird, and its cries drove the town into a panic.'

"Aren't any of you man enough to say something—not even behind the so-called Sheikh's back?

"Come on, show me now, which one of you is a real man? You, Razzouq? You, who laid into him with a cane? And what about you, who lifted him up—as a corpse?

"Speak up! Move! Or is the Sheikh's spittle stinging your tongues?

"God rest your soul, Radi, you died a man, while these chickenshits live on."

I didn't find my voice, but I found my tears. I found them reflected in my aunt's eyes when I caught sight of her ancient face under the cowl of her black abaya. My father's sister was too proud to wail, and her expression seemed prescient—of what, I didn't know. She held onto her daughter's hand who, after hearing Abbas, had begun to beat her chest and bite down on the corner of her abaya. Before, my aunt had held back her tears for Radi until his return. And she held them back again now, even though he had died in her arms, as if she refused to believe that someone like Radi could die. In the days between the two bouts of silent weeping, she had laughed until her back teeth showed, until it seemed she wasn't at all the aunt I knew. Her face looked like a stranger's to me, and especially so on the night he came home. He'd been almost a ghost then, trying to find his way through the dense clouds of palm-smoke from ovens baking the evening bread, and knocking on the broken-down door of his home, which was roofed with heavy palm trunks. Radi had knocked on a single door, but the exciting news had knocked on all ears. And in less time than it took for Radi to convince his family that he was their son, we were walking to the courtyard, stepping over the blood of the animal slaughtered in celebration.

That night, my aunt laughed and gave out all her coffee, pouring it into cups for us boys to serve to the men. Her voice—it was like I was hearing it for the first time—interrupted Radi as he told his strange story, "Oh, my heart and soul. Can I really believe my eyes?" It was hard for my aunt to believe her eyes, and it was hard for us to believe our eyes, too. Radi had been dead until an hour earlier, along with all the other Arab soldiers the Turks had sent off to the Caucasus. All we'd heard of them had been stories that reached us with a heavy dose of exaggeration. People said that whoever didn't die from the cold was murdered by one of his comrades, who wanted to steal his coat to ward off the sting of the freezing snow. And whoever didn't die from the cold, or as a victim of someone else who was feeling cold, died from hunger or hardship. We couldn't decide which of those deaths to choose for Radi, and—as for him—he had chosen not to die. And because he didn't want to die murdered, or from hunger or the cold, he remembered he had two feet and hung onto the tail end of a caravan that carried him, in disguise, from Tbilisi to Tabriz, then followed another from Tabriz to Tehran. He waited on the mounts and those who rode them until, two years later, after crossing a succession of borders, he was able to return to Iraq.

"Hammouda, light of my eyes," my aunt called out to me as she loaded me up with coffee cups, "Can I believe it? Have I truly lived to see Radi, right here in front of me?"

Believe it aunt, and hush now, I thought, let me listen to this, which is even stranger than the story of soldiers fighting each other to death over a coat. Can't you hear them asking, "And what did you see there, Radi?"

"What did I see? I saw plenty… marvels and more… things that were beyond marvelous." With long dark fingers, he picked up his second cup of coffee, nodding in every direction and swallowing another "I saw plenty" with every sip.

"By God, is that so? You don't say."

"Yes, I'm…" And he went quiet, like someone collecting his scattered thoughts, or thinking about where to begin, or holding back from saying things the others could only deny. "I saw iron coaches, each gripping the one in front of it. The leader pulled the others and moved them along on two shining straight hairs, like the straight and narrow path."

Eyes went round and opened their widest, the wonder in them spreading like pollen from one to the next. Radi's voice grew muffled as he took another sip, from yet another cup of coffee.

"… and that's not all. There were other things, even more marvelous! Small coaches that travel on every road, with eyes that light up and go dark, and room to carry five or six people. They race along, calling out, 'Baalek, baalek.'"

The thought that there might be any truth to these strange tales was too much for my aunt. Holding the coffee pot, she called out, "Radi, dear, I worry you were imagining things."

"No, I swear on my love for you, Ummi. And it wasn't just those—there was this big bird, bigger than a roc! Its screams drove the whole town into such a panic, you'd think the sky had collapsed onto the earth."

Our ears couldn't bear to hear about the sky collapsing onto the earth, and our pupils darted back and forth, giving away our unvoiced doubts—doubts that my aunt voiced in her own way.

"Be careful, light of my eyes, the Sheikh might hear you and say you've gone mad."

It was as if my aunt, by nature, had an incredible ability to perceive things, for the very next night, more than one of the Sheikh's followers crept in to sit with the group—each holding a cup of coffee and listening hard enough for ten ears. They said nothing, but their lips moved in constant low muttering. They kept asking God's forgiveness, until they got up to leave, and we thought they'd formed a judgment about Radi to take back to the Sheikh. It didn't matter what their conclusion was, be it blasphemy or madness—this Sheikh would have a cure. Yes, there was no affliction too great for the Sheikh, for his work was abundant and his blessings many and various. These were known by our sick, over whose heads he would read an invocation, which could be long or short depending on the remedy. They were known by our barren women, who came back from visiting him with a cure that made their wombs fertile, and by the mad among us, whose medicine was delivered with pomegranate-wood canes to drive away the ifrits. They were also known by our zealots, who he anointed as followers by spitting in the backs of their throats.

But who could have known what this Sheikh had in store for Radi? Sometimes, his methods involved more than just invocations, talismans, and canes, since some ifrits can't be cured with sticks. This type of spiritual possession rebels against violence and submits only to a gentle approach. Recently, we had seen the case of one of Abbas's sisters, a simple-minded girl who was neither beaten nor flogged. The Sheikh had a different manner of dealing with her ifrits… But before the whispers in the village gained traction, Abbas found a way to silence them, and he came out to us carrying a dripping red knife that had put an end to both possessor and possessed.

He's mad…

That was the Sheikh's verdict, and his head had seemed to shrink under his green turban as he listened to tales of the blasphemous creation that moved along on two hairs like the straight and narrow path, and of the iron coach calling "Baalek, baalek," and of the roc whose cries drove the town into a panic.

A madman raving with words the ifrits put on his lips.

"Razzouq!"

And Razzouq brought them—the canes made from branches of a pomegranate tree, soaked in water to make them supple. Four of the Sheikh's men came forward and tied Radi up, and then blows from the sticks rained down without delay.

"Twenty, then twenty more, and twenty more again."

But the ifrits were undeterred, and there was no lull in their ravings.

"They move along two hairs like the straight and narrow path? Twenty more.

"It calls, 'Baalek?' Twenty.

"And bigger —you say— bigger than a roc? Twenty for this one. No, forty…"

The sticks continued to follow their orders, and the truth continued to roar out through the man's mouth until he stopped being a madman or an infidel.

They carried him to my aunt, a corpse.

Barely a week later, the news reports started up, and hardly an hour went by without one. The Turkish garrison had withdrawn from the outskirts of Shahraban, and we heard, at gatherings in the local inns, that the British were advancing north. One night, someone came to us saying that, about a five-hour walk to the south, he saw two hairs, yes, two hairs shining like vipers. A little later, he remembered the Sheikh's sticks and denied what he'd said. The next morning, we heard another man say the same. And, in the evening, there was someone who swore he saw iron coaches crawling along the ground. Yesterday, we all saw them, circling the town and spewing out dark-skinned Indians and red-faced soldiers. And today, before we finally believed we weren't dreaming, the town was driven into a panic by the roc birds filling our skies and tearing our ears apart with a sound like thunder.

Our muddy group swelled with townspeople—furtive, silent, and despondent. In the absence of speech, words hammered into our minds: it was as if the idea flowed from head to head through wires made of silence. Abbas's eyes burned red as coals. Under her abaya, my aunt's eyes poured out pure hate, and her daughter bit down on the corner of her own abaya to silence the wails that wanted to escape her mouth. The palm trees above us shook, as if rocked by a soundless howling, and our lips went stiff as we struggled against our choking emotions. Except where people clustered tightly, our shadows lay long on the ground.

Abbas took a single step forward and signaled to me, so I started walking, too.

We walked without looking back, but I sensed a shadow behind me—following my own—then a third, a fourth, and a fifth.

Bare feet shuffled forward on the furrowed mud, and shadows chased each other as the group crammed in together.

We formed a caravan that knew its route, and we made our way toward him, bearing a certain judgment —a judgment borne even by the followers of that Sheikh, those anointed with spit in the backs of their throats.

THE PASSENGER

When I looked up at the list of scheduled arrivals and departures displayed in the middle of Beirut Airport's spacious lobby, I was surprised to find that my sister's flight from Cairo wouldn't arrive until six, and that I'd have to wait a whole hour and fifteen minutes.

Had the airline employee made a mistake with the time? Had I misheard him? Or had the flight's departure from Cairo been delayed for some reason?

I didn't know, but with all the overcrowding in the lobby, terrace, and bar, the job of waiting didn't seem like a pleasant one. Even trying to read the magazine I was holding seemed pointless amidst the commotion that filled the air.

There was one flight taking off for Brazil, another about to land from Kuwait, and a third just arriving from Baghdad. People were greeting arrivals and saying farewells, smiling or crying, some sharing their emotions openly while others were reserved, holding back, and still others seemed to be the type not to show their feelings unless forced to do so for the sake of basic courtesy or social hypocrisy.

My gaze wandered as I looked for a quiet corner, but I decided instead to go out onto the terrace to watch the far-off airplane; it was about to relax its wings to land on the vast runway where it would slowly, majestically, taxi to a halt.

Many eyes were glued to the plane—the eyes of mothers and wives and siblings and friends—all full of barely contained anticipation.

The plane landed, its doors opened, and passengers began to descend the short metal staircase. I found that my curiosity stopped here, and my eyes now needed a new distraction to keep them occupied.

I had just moved my foot, intending to walk off, when a crowd of people poured out onto the terrace. It was clear from their strange mishmash of outfits that they weren't from the city. I didn't know whether they were there to see off a loved one, or rushing to greet passengers from the recently landed plane, but they had the kind of eagerness that people from the country, unlike those from the city, never manage to bury under layers of fake composure. I didn't have to wonder for long. When I let my curiosity loose again, my gaze landed on tearful eyes, and my ears picked up one of their voices saying, "The one for Brazil's parked over there, at the far end of the runway."

So they were seeing someone off, but who?

I returned my attention to the group, searching for someone who looked like a passenger, but the camera one of them was holding saved me the effort. He was aiming it at a short man wearing a dress shirt and kaleidoscopic necktie, where twenty colors vied for space. With a once-white—but now visibly yellowing—straw hat on his head, he stood in the middle of the terrace, facing the sun. Next to him was a man in black sirwal-style pants, which narrowed at the knee and disappeared into black shoes that had never seen a lick of polish. He wore a khaki keffiyeh wrapped around his head. The man in the hat reached out, as if to shake hands with the man standing beside him, and the camera took the shot.

After that, the man in the black sirwal moved away and an old woman took his place. She hooked her withered arm around the short man's neck and, dragging him closer, began to sob, saying, "Go on, son, take the picture. Take a picture that will eat my heart every time I see it."

The cameraman took one photo, then a second and a third, but the old woman couldn't be persuaded to change her pose.

The other women in the group burst out crying, lifting handkerchiefs to their eyes to soak up their tears, and the men began to scold them. One man decided to take a different approach and, instead of scolding, said, "Stop it now, no tears. It's bad karma to cry! People travel all the time. It takes a real man to live abroad."

But the women didn't stop. Their tears flowed in buckets every time they saw Farahat turn to the camera as he hugged a man or woman from the group, saying, "Take a photo of me with Hana as a keepsake… with Bu Masoud as a keepsake… and a keepsake with…"

The camera took photos of Farahat with everyone all together, and with each of them separately, and then its job was done. He raised his hat and then, taking a small bottle of arak from Bu Masoud's hand, he greedily swigged from it while toasting the group with a loud, "To your health!"

Farahat's merriment went on until it was interrupted by the loudspeaker calling, in three languages, for passengers traveling to Brazil to proceed to security, and then to customs control to complete their travel procedures.

"Yalla, I guess this is it, Farahat. Good luck."

Farahat turned to look at his entourage, his eyes red, then he hurled himself back to the old woman, kissing her hand. Perhaps she was his mother? She must have been his mother—she had pulled off his hat and kept kissing his head, unable to stop. She only stepped back when someone reached out a strong hand to Farahat and said, "Come on now, Farahat, pull yourself together man. Let's go, everyone."

Then the kisses grew louder and colorful handkerchiefs came out again to sop up the tears. Heavy sweat poured from Farahat's hands and face, and he only managed to pry himself free when an airline employee came to warn him that he needed to hurry up.

The man dragged himself on his way, so drunk that his feet could barely carry him to where the security officers were sitting. The circle of well-wishers stayed behind on the terrace, waiting until he was finished so they could watch him as he walked to the plane.

I stood where I was. The emotional scene had begun to affect me, but I didn't want to lose my composure in such a public place, so I tried to distract myself from Farahat's group by focusing on other things. I soon turned back, though, and saw the old woman craning her neck to look for her son through the glass window of the ground-floor lounge, where the passengers gathered before the flight attendant guided them to the plane.

I, too, found myself thinking about Farahat, trying, from what I'd seen, to work out who from the group could be his mother, his brothers and his sisters, and the children of his brothers and sisters. This might not be his first trip to Brazil, especially since his head had found its way into a hat. Maybe an adventuring ship had once taken him on board, along with his dreams of life in a land where stories said the soil was full of gold and diamonds. Maybe he had traveled and stayed there, one of thousands devoured by loneliness who could only console themselves with hard work, so that their sorrow in the comfortless nights would be chewed up by the grind of daily labor.

Maybe Farahat had married a woman from there who didn't understand why her husband cried every time he sat down with his children at the Eid table, or at his friend's house when he heard a record, where the scratches were muffled by Umm Kulthum's voice singing, "I'd give my life for him, no matter what. Whether he cherishes our love or gives it up."

Maybe, when Farahat got angry and let out a stream of blasphemous curses, or filled the air with words they didn't understand, his children and their Brazilian mother would just laugh and laugh. So many maybes…

I kept looking at Umm Farahat. That poor woman. Perhaps the grief of her son's absence had ruined her enjoyment of the taste of raw kibbeh, pounded in a ringing mortar, and the sweetness of the jar of grape molasses she'd preserved to stave off the lean months of winter.

For her, history began and ended with something from and for Farahat.

The fig tree had become generous from the day her beloved son had traveled, and the fat sheep was slaughtered the day he wrote to tell her he'd married a woman from over there. His spirit lingered in the house and under the grapevine, and his scent filled every breath of good fortune that blew into their home.

She was still crying when I glanced up again, still struggling to crane her neck as she searched for him among the passengers.

But he saved her the trouble when he came out onto the tarmac.

In his right hand, he held a basket, carrying it with obvious care, and in his left, he clutched the large handkerchief he was using to dry his sweat.

He stood out on the tarmac, letting his well-wishers have their fill of him.

"Don't forget us, Farahat! Farahat, my precious boy, who will bury me if I die while you're gone? Farahat, kiss the children… Teach them to love us… Bring them with you next time… Farahat, Farahat, Farahat…"

Farahat stood frozen, not knowing what to do, looking at his mother and saying nothing.

The old woman looked as if she was about to throw herself down onto him from the airport terrace.

I raised my hand to brush away the tears from under my black sunglasses and fought the temptation to wave back when Farahat turned to leave, holding onto his basket and lifting his hat in a feeble wave with every ten steps he took.

And when he climbed up and stood on the stairs, the runway was strewn with the village's emotions, and his mother threw her heart into the plane.

I had turned away to dry my eyes when I was surprised by a friend, who tapped me on the shoulder and said, "Hey! Are you picking someone up?"

"No," I said, "I'm… I'm seeing Farahat off. He's flying to Brazil!"

ANOTHER YEAR

In one of the lines of cars waiting to be inspected at the Daraa customs crossing, an old woman sat hunched under a gray blanket. Starting to fret a little, she began to look around, peering through the rear window at a blond Syrian inspector as he ran his eyes over the bags, then stuck out a finger to poke through the contents of a suitcase that could never have been closed without the rope it was tied with. The old woman tapped on the glass, and the driver walked over. "What do those people want from us, Son?" she asked.

"Nothing, they're just doing their job. They'll let us go as soon as they're done."

"Did they meddle with the basket?"

"They asked me what was in it, so I said: boiled eggs, date-filled cookies, pine nuts, and... You must have counted off the contents in front of me at least ten times, right?"

"You forgot the coffee beans, Son. Coffee is precious over there, it's worth more than gold! I brought two kilos of it for Mary. She loves coffee, you see. She used to practically open her eyes in the morning with a match in hand to light the Primus. She'd make coffee and bring some to me and her brothers and sisters, and then she'd drink the rest of the pot herself.

"Ah..." she sighed, using a corner of her black shawl to wipe a tear from the crevices of her ancient face.

The inspection was done, and the driver returned to his seat. Adjusting his woolen skull cap, he started the engine and then they were off, the car making its way along the desert road that led to the Jordanian border crossing.

"How long till we get there?" asked the old woman, raising stiff, scrawny fingers to draw the sign of the cross over her face three times.

The driver answered without taking his eyes off the road: "It's one in the afternoon now—we might make it to Amman by six this evening if everything goes well and we're not delayed by the Jordanian police inspection at Al-Ramtha."

"Will they inspect our luggage, too?"

"They must. It's their duty."

"In that case, Son, try not to let them open the basket. Tell them I've packed a few things in it for Mary: boiled eg—"

"Boiled eggs, date-filled cookies, pine nuts, and coffee."

"And apples and some clothes, children's clothes. A suit for Karim and another just like it for Elias, and a red jacket for Abdel Nour. I don't know why, but Abdel Nour is my favorite of the three boys. Maybe because he's named for his grandfather—Abboud's father? Abdel Nour was born a year ago over Christmas. We found out from the radio that Mary had delivered her baby. I didn't hear the message myself, a friend heard, and she told me the news. I kissed the ground twice in thanks for her safety. Three deliveries with no family nearby. Her mother-in-law is dead, and her mother, alas, lives far away. It's seven years since we parted; she was a bride when I left her, and now she's mother to Karim, Elias, and Abdel Nour.

"Seven years… It's a lifetime, my son, a lifetime. She couldn't come from Nazareth to Jerusalem to see us because she was always either pregnant or had just given birth. One year, her husband came, so my son Abboud went to meet him in Jerusalem. He told Abboud that his sister had grown thin, and gray hairs had crept onto her head. Poor thing, it's too early for her to go gray. How old is she to be going gray so soon? Girls her age are still single. She's only just shy of twenty-six, two years younger than Abboud, and he's not even married yet, but Mary has three sons: Karim and—"

"—and Elias and Abdel Nour. And the little one is named after his grandfather, and—"

"Bless you, Son, you have a strong memory! It's youth. Ah, youth. Before I grew old and bent, I knew by heart the important dates for every member of our community: when they were born, when they were married, when they died. They called me the parish register. How different I am now from the girl I was back then. Heartache dulls the mind, Son, and wears away one's health. We used to live in Jaffa. Do you know Jaffa?

"Our house was in Daraj Al Qalaa. We had an orange grove there, and our fruit shone like gold and was famous for its sweetness. We were a good family, and our house was like a hotel, welcoming to all. My husband was the mukhtar, you see, and our custom says the mukhtar must offer hospitality to visiting strangers. We were constantly cooking and fanning the flames, and there were always visitors coming and going. The day Mary got married, we had twenty or more sleeping at our house. There was more than enough bedding, and plenty of food to go around… And we had those copper pots that Abboud's grandfather bought in Damascus. And then the house went, and the orange grove went, and the bedding, and the copper pots—everything went. Now I own two mattresses, two pots, and a table that Abboud made before he went to the desert. And I live in a single room."

"Ehh, such is life."

"Slow down, Son, you're making my bones hurt. What are those buildings? Are we there?"

"This isn't Amman, it's Al-Ramtha."

"Oh. This is where they inspect us?"

The car came to a stop, and the driver jumped out, taking everyone's passports with him for the customs officers to check. With some effort, the old woman wound down the window and stuck out her head for some fresh air. She called to the copper-skinned policeman in the red keffiyeh and spoke to him in a near-whisper. "That basket in the trunk belongs to me, Son. Let me save you the trouble of searching it by telling you it has boiled eggs in it and—"

"Boiled eggs?"

"Yes, I'm traveling to meet Mary; she's coming from Nazareth to Jerusalem. I thought that boiled eggs—"

"But Mary might want them fried, so why did you boil them?"

The old woman curled her wrinkled lips into an ancient smile and said, "I was thinking ahead. I told myself that raw eggs wouldn't make it there in one piece. With all the shaking and rattling, they'd break and leak onto the cookies and the pine nuts and the clothes. They say clothes are pricey there, Son, have you heard that, too? And there are no eggs to be found at all, that's what I heard from the people who went to Jerusalem last year. And meat is hard to come by, too. I would have liked to bring her some meat, but I was afraid it would rot. It doesn't matter if food is scarce, Son, it's being safe and healthy that counts. And as long as Mary and her husband and children are well, I thank God a thousand times. We're better off than others, and there are others better off than us. Money can be replaced, and homes can come back to us as long as our men are still standing. As for the tyrants, their day of reckoning will come. When Abboud looks in on me at home, I forget the tears, the hardship, and the never-ending heartache. The only thing that grieves me is being parted from my Mary. Seven years, Son.

I left her when she was a bride, and now she's mother to Karim, Elias, and Abdel Nour."

The old woman caught sight of the driver returning and swallowed the rest of her words. Pulling her head back into the car, she rearranged the blanket and began to nibble at a cookie she had taken out of her bag. "Ya Karim," she sighed, praying for God's grace, and the car started on its way.

"Son, do you know where Jubran Al-Sayegh's house is in Amman?"

"No."

"You must know where it is. How else can you claim you go to Amman every other day? Jubran owns a fabric store on… oh, I forgot the name of the street. Wait a minute while I look for the address. Abboud wrote it down for me on a piece of paper. Ah yes, here you are. Read it. Take me to his house, I'm spending the night there. We're related to him by marriage, and his wife's been Mary's friend since they went to convent school together, they're about the same age. Do you think his store will still be open when we get there? Why aren't you answering me? You must be tired. You've a right to be. My bones are killing me from just one trip, and God only knows how I'd feel if I had to make three trips a week like you do. I never would have considered going all this way if I didn't have to. But I'd have walked the whole way rather than miss this. If you were a father, you'd recognize a mother's longing. There is nothing dearer than one's children, Son, except one's children's children. My heart is soaring and all I want is for this night to pass quickly, and to find a car with a nice driver like you to take me to Jerusalem. I can't wait to kiss Mary, and smell her—I'll never get my fill of her. And I'll ask her questions till my mouth runs dry. I'll ask her about Jaffa, maybe she's been back since we left. I wonder what's become of our house. Is it still standing? Who is still there from our people, and who has fled? And our orchard, has she tasted its oranges again? And the church? Is Father Ibrahim still pastor there? And my friends, Sarah, Umm Jamil, and Mariana, are they still daughters of this world?"

Umm Abboud began to tell the life stories of Sarah, Umm Jamil, and Mariana. She had barely finished the third when her head dropped onto her shoulder, and she dozed off, sleeping until the driver shook her awake when the car arrived at Jubran's store. Startled, she opened her eyes and sat up straight, looking behind her to make sure the basket was safe.

In Jerusalem, in front of the Mandelbaum gate, Umm Abboud sits on a rock, almost lost amidst the sea of faces, the cries of street-vendors, the clamoring of crowds, and the calls of rosary bearers. She is a small figure, hardly visible between the piles of religious pictures and necklaces. Faces full of longing pass by her as if they were all one single face: eyes searching and heads craning over shoulders. Suddenly, those arriving from the stolen land come into view as they step onto Jordanian soil and are snatched up by the eagerness of the waiting ones. Sobs mingle as two heads embrace. When will Mary's turn come? Who comes first? The Jaffans, the Nazarenes, or the Haifans? Mary mustn't be late because the old woman's strength has run out: her legs are tired, her mouth is dry, and she is beginning to feel hungry.

"Hey, you," she says, grabbing a villager standing in front of her by the hem of his robe. "Step aside! I want to see Mary—Mary, my daughter, who's coming from Nazareth. If you hear anyone asking for Umm Abboud, lead them to me. If it wasn't for this basket, I would have squeezed through to the front of the lines. Who can bear to wait when Mary, her husband, and her three boys are right behind the barrier?"

The shouting grows louder. Umm Abboud's voice joins the clamor, and people's calls mingle together. Eyes scan the area, searching for their loved ones. Tears and kisses, kisses and tears, and rising gasps of joy. And Mary, there's no sign of Mary. Why is she late? "Haven't they let the Nazarenes through yet? When will their turn come, Uncle? You say they've come out already? No, they're not out yet, or else where's my Mary? If any of you see Mary, tell her that her mother's waiting for her… Have you seen her? She's neither tall nor short and has honey-colored hair and light skin. She has a man and three boys with her. Mary, Mary, Mary."

She came out of her fainting spell to find a man from Nazareth by her side. Mary had tasked him with passing on her greetings to her mother: her husband had fallen ill, and she'd asked the man to soften the blow of her absence by promising Umm Abboud that she would come to meet her the following year.

The old woman stammered out her words as she wiped her tears with the corner of her black shawl. "T-t-take the basket then, Uncle, take it. The dresses are for her, the woolen undershirts are for her husband, and the rest is for the children. The red jacket is for Abdel Nour. Take it and kiss her on the head for me. Give her my greetings and tell her I said that, if I live another year, I'll crawl here on all fours to see her. And if God takes me before then, I will die with grief in my heart for only two things: grief for my country and grief for Mary and the kiss I ached to plant on her cheek."

ZAGHARID

A few days earlier, someone came and told Salma Al-Sawwaf that the Near East Arab Radio Station, which broadcast letters from refugees to their families, had aired the following message, directed at her:

"From Jamil Abdullah in Beirut to his father Karim Abdullah, his mother Salma, and his sister Wedad in Jaffa: I am well and so is my fiancée, Nadia. We will be married at 3 p.m. on the 8th of May in the Church of Our Lady, and then we'll travel to Kuwait, where I'll be working. We miss you, send us your news on the radio."

Salma and her husband couldn't hold back their tears when, a few days later, the radio relayed their answer:

"From Karim Abdullah, his wife Salma, his daughter Wedad, and her husband: Congratulations on your wedding. We wish you all the best."

That was the most Salma and Karim could do for Jamil's wedding. They had looked forward to this special occasion ever since Jamil had come into the world—ever since then, none of their visitors would finish their coffee without wishing them, "The joy of celebrating Jamil's wedding, God willing."

It had never occurred to Salma that she might be deprived of a place at the wedding, not unless death caught up with her first, or fate stopped her from going.

It wasn't as if Beirut was in India or China: the trip to Beirut would take no more than six hours by car or half an hour by plane. But it was impossible—no, beyond impossible—for her to taste the joy of her lifetime and feast her eyes on the sight of Jamil as a bridegroom, his soft hair shining under a wedding crown hung with white ribbons. The priest would place the crown on Jamil's head and another just like it on the bride's head, and then he'd bury his face in his book and chant aloud:

"Oh Lord, bless them with fruit of the womb and the goodness of procreation, grant them harmony in body and soul, give them bountiful harvests so they may have sufficiency in all things and so they may gaze upon their grandchildren, like young olive shoots around their table."

How can life be so cruel that there's not a grain of mercy to be had for a mother's heart, nor a moment of joy for a father's?

Salma's eyes are locked on the clock; she can barely make out the clock-hands through her tears. Nearby, Abu Jamil moves around restlessly: standing up, sitting down, spitting out of the window, and cursing the hell out of the Israelis. Salma's daughter Wedad is there, too, along with her husband and children.

The clock strikes three, and Umm Jamil bursts into tears as she looks through the window down the length of the deserted, almost lifeless street; no boys being rowdy, no girls playing, no old men basking in the sunshine on stools in front of their houses. They've all either died, or gone away, or been abandoned by prosperity.

Now, at this precise moment, Jamil will have taken his bride's hand as they walk together to the altar, preceded by a priest with an incense burner. The guests will be pushing forward to get a look at the bride. But what does this bride look like, Salma wonders? Fair or dark? Tall or short? She'd never been introduced to her, not even in a photo or a letter. Is she pretty enough to deserve Jamil? Is she a good woman, worthy of being the mother of his children?

From what Salma knows of him, he likes the pretty ones—he could always pick them out when he was younger, when he used to come from Beirut every summer to spend the school holidays with her. Out of all the girls, she had wanted her cousin's daughter for him: she was as pretty as a doll and had the upbringing of a girl from a good family. Every time, when she joked around with Jamil, she'd encouraged him to work hard to become an engineer and promised that his bride would arrive at his home just a week after he graduated. But how times had changed! The wheels of fortune had turned, and the ties between her and her loved ones had been cut. She'd been deprived of Jamil's visits, and—ever since her sister's whole family, and her cousins, and her husband's sisters had all emigrated—she had also been denied the affection and company of relatives. Salma had stayed in Jaffa because her husband was ill, and her daughter had chosen to stay because her husband was wise. But Jamil had remained in Beirut, far away, while she stayed on with the others who had stayed, being force-fed humiliation and living on the memories that came to her with each new surge of emotions that circumstances stirred up.

Jamil is being married right now! If only she had wings to fly to him. He was being married with no mother or father by his side… How lonely he must be when there isn't a single member of his family there with him. Everybody there is from her family: her mother, her father, her brothers and sisters, her relatives. One of them will witness the marriage, that's for sure. She had hoped one of his paternal cousins would be a witness, a young man whose veins pulsed with the same blood as Jamil's. How could he get married like this, as if he'd been cut away from the family tree?

Umm Jamil grew even more upset when she was hit by a sudden wave of hatred for the bride's family: they had caught Jamil in their nets and rushed him into marriage. They hadn't let him wait until the restrictions were eased and the crisis had died down.

And what was this church they had chosen for him to get married in? Was it as big as St George's in Jaffa? Did it stand, like St George's, stately, upright and majestic, with the smells of incense and burnt candle wax wafting through an atmosphere of purity and prayer? How Jaffa yearned to see the wedding of one of its sons! Even weddings had become beggars' funerals. The taste of happiness had died in people's mouths and grief had been branded on their foreheads.

Would they celebrate Jamil's wedding, her only son's wedding, the way weddings are meant to be celebrated? With a churchyard full of guests, and the wedding family generously handing out sugared almonds that everyone—young and old—would eat, and then pray for the bride and groom's prosperity? Who would receive congratulations after the ceremony? Her mother and father? And which of the guests was keen enough on tradition to remember the needle and thread to sew the bride's dress to the groom's suit, to keep alive a custom that mothers hold dear to their hearts?

Jamil is feeling shy, no doubt, and drowning in a sea of sweat. She would give her life to see him in his black wedding suit. Was he thinking of her now, wishing she and his father were there with him? Did he miss hearing her voice amidst the clamoring zagharid?

Who was trilling out zagharid in honor of the groom? The bride's mother? Brazenly, as if it was her own son's wedding? God damn her! With Salma out of the way, she had them all to herself; she was both his mother and her mother. She could ask for whatever she wanted. If only Salma were nearby, she would have stopped that woman and put a lid on her scheming ambitions—she knew all about the mothers of brides.

How long had it been since the wedding ceremony started? Half an hour? So by now the bride and groom would be following the priest in the usual circle around the altar, while the people chanted, "Crown them with glory and honor," and her son's forehead poured with sweat. The bride had nothing to do with her though, and she certainly wouldn't wonder what she might look like.

Salma wipes her eyes with the cuff of her sleeve and looks at her perplexed granddaughters, who are holding the unlit candles she'd given them. She yells at them, "Your candles are out and it's your uncle's wedding? I'll make those flames dance for joy, or my name isn't Salma. Light the candles, children, light them and smile! Why are your faces stiff as statues? Jamil doesn't get married every day, does he? And it's not every day that a bride's lucky enough to marry a groom like him, is it? Come here and chant like this... What? Don't you love Jamil? Why don't you open your mouths and sing a wedding hymn?"

She went closer to the girls to light their candles, but they didn't move. They gaped at her with strange expressions as she wove back and forth between them, wiping her tears on the sleeve of her dress and shaking the neighborhood's gloomy silence with her strangled zagharid.

ON THE WAY TO SOLOMON'S POOLS

He knew the battle was unequal. His bullets were charged with hatred, but all they would trigger was a new downpour of destruction. And he knew it was foolish to shoot. His machine gun was a child's toy in the face of the relentless shelling, but he'd been trying to cover the fleeing residents. They had begun to leave their village that afternoon, realizing that by staying when their bullets had run out, they were at best playing a game of suicide. Once he and his brothers-in-arms from the National Guard had gone over their plans and worked out that their ammunition would last only a few more hours, he'd made a pact with a few of them to cover the villagers' retreat. Their village, Battir, sat on a hillside leading down to the valley that separated them from the Jewish bases on the mountain to the west. A railway line cut through the valley, cleaving the village in two and splitting off the school and a few houses from the more densely built-up area on the hillside. He and his friends on the other rooftops hoped, with their bullets, to bluff the Jewish fighters into thinking they had ammunition to back their defense—a short-lived ploy that was about to end when he fired his last shot.

It was a moonlit night. The flowers of the almond and apricot trees in his garden, and in the orchards beyond, were bathed in luster, so that they became tiny white stars, turning the night into poetry. The starry blossoms were like innocent eyes, looking on unaware as tragedy unfolded.

In front of him, behind the railway tracks, he saw the school where he used to teach. It seemed a hollow husk, mocking the lively spirit he'd tried to instill in his young companions, and mocking the stories he'd told them each day, before their morning exercises. He used to stand among them and say, "Look over at that mountain! One day, we will make it an Arab mountain." And all eyes would turn to the west and look up to trace the mountain's hills and its sun-kissed peak.

His wife stood behind him, encouraging him to stay strong as she tried to overcome her terror of the flaring missiles.

He fired his last bullet. The prattle of cannon fire responded, and he felt the stone bricks of his house being shaken loose by the blasts. He threw away his machine gun: without bullets, it was only a toy.

This couldn't be the end! There must be something he could do! Earlier, at noon, someone had come to assure him that boxes of ammunition were on their way to Battir. But afternoon, sunset, and evening had come and gone, and nothing had shown up.

If the ammunition had arrived in time, his comrades from the Young Guards would have towered like giants on every rooftop. But his friend Ahmed had gone round to all the neighboring villages and found only old rifles, with no bullets except the ones they were loaded with. A rifle against a cannon? It was a dwarf against a giant.

Pacing the rooftop, his nails digging into his palms, he felt that nothing made a man more impotent than facing a barrage of fire. He looked at his wife. She was crying. For the first time, she was afraid, as if the empty machine gun had convinced her that Hassan's heroism was nothing but childish antics, and that the lines of young men he'd worked hard to train were mere dolls in the hands of a trifling child. Didn't he have anything to offer his wife? No hint of reassurance that might give her some peace of mind?

He felt that his empty machine gun, that useless stick, had dealt his manhood a humiliating blow. Without bullets, he would die a mouse's death in his own home.

It troubled him that Souad was crying. He glared at her, but all she said was, "What about our son, Hassan?"

Omar? It was for Omar's sake that he was fighting. It was for a whole generation of Omar's friends—the children of this country—that he was a teacher by day and carried a gun at night.

So yes, what about his son? The answer lay with the barricades that didn't have enough fighters, and the fighters who didn't have enough ammunition. His imagination swam with images of a troop celebrating a despicable victory.

He looked at his wife: either he died here, with her and Omar, or they could head for Solomon's Pools with the others who'd been forced to abandon their homes. He would leave the child and his mother there, and then he'd come back here to do something...

"Come on." He pulled her by the hand, and they climbed down the stairs together. He went to Omar's bed and picked him up. The child was asleep. Perhaps he was dreaming of a happy new day, where the sun rose in hope and set in tranquility, while he lay safe in his mother's arms.

He watched as his wife opened the closet, stuffed some clothes into a bundle, and then moved toward the nightstand to pick up their wedding picture.

They set off, his wife carrying the bundle while he carried Omar, clutching him gently to his chest, trying desperately to keep him warm so he wouldn't be scared, nor open his eyes onto a night of terror. The buzz of the bullets had died down, as had the roaring cannons. Maybe the Jewish fighters had finally realized it was pointless to waste bullets on a defenseless village. Perhaps they had sat down to rest, or to draw up a plan for their advance, which was made all the easier because they were descending on Battir from the mountain, and it lay weak and exposed, on the side of the valley.

Hassan turned back to look at his house. It was still standing, tall and dignified. Awash in the fragrance of spring's plentiful almond blossoms, its white walls soaked up the silver rays of the moon. The stones of his house came from the nearby mountain's quarries, and his garden had been sown with a mattock, its every strike bringing forth a thousand pledges.

He had planted the almond tree on the day Omar was born, and the sapling had blossomed and grown. He used to stand Omar next to it and say, "Let's see who's taller now—you or the almond tree?"

He saw his wife look back as well. Their eyes met, and, in a single moment, they recalled a lifetime of emotions. It had all begun when he met her as a student in Jerusalem. He'd fallen in love with her and brought her here, to this house. Together, side by side, they had planted the garden, filling it with flowers and trees, and filling their home with love and contentment. Yes, this was their home, their tender nest. There was a story behind every stone in its walls.

Souad let out a muffled sob.

But he tried to hold himself together, drawing courage from the warmth of the soft little body he held.

They started walking faster.

The road was empty. The houses were as still as gravestones in an ancient cemetery, free of any signs of life except the trees.

Bullets thundered again. He yelled at his wife to hit the ground as he crouched down low. They stayed like that for a few moments until the bullets stopped, and then they got up. Hassan looked around, trying to figure out which direction the shots were coming from, but stopped short as a missile shattered the night's silence. He screamed, "Run!"

They ran together. And kept on running for more than twenty minutes, until he felt his wife was exhausted, so he slowed down. He lifted his left hand to ease its stiffness and felt something hot wash over it.

Had he been hit? Turning his hand over, he saw no trace of a bullet wound and felt no pain. He trembled... Was it Omar?

He smothered his reaction. The slightest wrong move would paralyze his wife: He didn't dare stop to see where the blood was coming from in case she became suspicious.

Pulling the small body closer, he began to walk, moving too fast for his wife to keep up.

The gap between them grew wider, and he heard her calling. Her voice carried, sounding sad and afraid. "I'm here," he choked out, without looking back.

Waiting until she drew nearer, he started walking again, desperate to get away, as her voice came at him from behind, "You must be tired of carrying the little one. Give him to me."

He was weeping, so he didn't answer, didn't turn toward her voice, which slapped at his back. "The wind is getting colder," she said. "Take this blanket and wrap it around Omar."

Without letting her see his face, he took the blanket, wrapped his son in it, and ran.

He ran away from her voice as she called out to him. If she found out the truth, she would drop down dead. Let her find her way on her own, with the rest of those fleeing their homes. Turning right, he ventured deep into a narrow path, stopped, and lifted the blanket. He tilted back the small body, which was erupting with blood.

A surge of emotions choked him, a fusion of pain, hatred, and bitterness.

Gently, lovingly, he set the child down on the soil. The moon had sunk lower and taken on reddish hues, as if it were a sun rising from the west. And, as a ribbon of magical dawn lights brightened the sky, the rooftops of the houses in Solomon's Pools appeared to him, square and flat.

He fell on the tender face, kissing it, talking to his son, calling him until his voice stuck in his throat and his tears were dried by the inferno that burned in his eyes. Again and again, he shook the little one, trying to restore the miracle of life. But not a stir came from the half-shut eyelids that drooped over eyes once vibrant with life—a life for whose sake he had planted that almond tree and carried that rifle.

He looked around, then turned toward the almond orchards. For a long moment, he let his eyes roam as he chose a lavishly garlanded tree, then lay the child down beneath it. He grappled with a branch, broke it off, and used it to dig, moving it around in a circle to make a hole that was soon wide enough for a tiny grave. Handful by handful, he covered his child with soil, then stood up and shook the tree so it spread a shroud of flowers over the grave, scattering it with white stars.

No prayer passed his lips, for hatred had stolen his voice.

Tearing himself from the grave, he started walking, pushing his way through the last of those who were fleeing, trying to steady himself so he didn't trip on the rocks in the road. Folded over his arm was a small, sticky blanket. He knew that, two hours ago, it hadn't been red.

WHEN HAJJ MOHAMMED SOLD OUT HIS HAJJ

To her, the woman in Beit Safafa I asked, from behind the fence, "How do you feel in your prison?"
"Tell me instead," she said, "how do you feel in your 'freedom'?" And with that answer-question, she stuffed a rock in my mouth.
S.

With one probing look, Salman Abu Akef read far more into it than he should have. He decided there must be a connection between the sight of Hajj Mohammed perched on a low stool, looking blankly into the distance, and the hill of empty bottles piled messily in the backyard of the white stone house, their colors eaten away by dust. Shaking his head, Salman spoke from behind the keffiyeh that permanently hid part of his face: "Hajj Mohammed has sold out his hajj!"

The village seized on this explanation of Hajj Mohammed's tragic silence, accepting it with little discussion, since his bereavement would surely express itself differently from the desperation of others whose sons had been killed, or wounded, or had ventured too far east. Hajj Mohammed's grief needed to erupt into something more intense than the silence that had possessed him, more significant than the look in his vacant eyes that clung to a horizon always blooming with surprises, and wept, without tears, for Faris—Faris, whose body, notched with ten bullets, lay under a gravestone that could deflect no one's pain.

People had become addicted to grief, and death seemed a logical, acceptable, and happy ending for everyone, no matter their age. The dead died once, and their deaths were certain and final; they knew why they had died, and they didn't have to live wondering what they were living for, with their voices smothered by roaring tractors that sliced open the stolen land behind the barbed wire fence. The grief of the living was drenched in sunlight, and they had to grieve with their eyes wide open.

"Hajj Mohammed sold out his hajj!"

This thought, like any other, had flitted across his friend Salman Abu Akef's mind. In the past, when such an idea had presented itself to Salman, he'd taken it to the diwan—where the men of the village held council—and discussed it there with his friends. But the diwan was no more; it, too, had been gobbled up by the fence and was now an Israeli police station. Meanwhile, Hajj Mohammed sat, as he did every day, with the bottles piling up in the yard behind him near a dust-covered trough and a cauldron that had turned black and green. He had recruited four boys to collect the bottles, paying them a millime or two for each one they brought in. But what was he doing with the bottles?

All it took to work that out was a clever man like Salman Abu Akef. Hajj Mohammed had begun collecting the bottles after three men had forced him to promise that he would harvest the grapes from his remaining vineyards—the ones left on this side of the fence—instead of leaving them to be eaten by wasps or scattered by November's winds. They had made him swear on Faris's grave to do something about it, and they had refused to leave until he made this memorable promise—memorable because it was one of the few words he had spoken for months.

"Hajj Mohammed has sold out his hajj!"

Now you know the secret behind the bottles, Salman, so pull your keffiyeh tight and go stir up the mire of your people's grief.

He has sold out his hajj—yes, he's betrayed all seven of them, one after the other. Four times, he had performed the hajj on his own, and Umm Faris had gone with him on the fifth. And on the sixth and seventh trips, he had taken along two poor men, and he'd dedicated one hajj to his father's soul and the other to his mother's. Seven pilgrimages! They were more like seven weddings, and each time—if you remember, Hajj—the village outdid itself on your return. They decked the streets with bunting in your honor, and dozens of sheep were driven to their fate, walking past with bent heads before ending up mounted on great hills of rice, in a feast laid out for every passerby.

When he returned to the village, the fence had been erected, and the armistice committee had eaten up part of his land. From one hundred dunams of eastern vineyards, barely twenty were left to him, and from two hundred dunams of terraced vineyards on the foothills, not more than forty remained. As for the Al-Zainy vineyard, the fence had taken it all. Knowing this, he had intended never to return, like so many migrating birds with weary wings who laid down to roost wherever they landed. But Faris's body, with its ten bullet holes, kept calling him back. He had to have a gravestone.

What had worried Hajj Mohammed most was that the fence might have eaten away the small marker he had put down before he left: four white stones that measured out two meters of land, not more than thirty steps away from the barricade. This was where Faris's friends had wanted him buried—not in the cemetery with those who had died in their beds, but rather here, near the barricade, where he used to shoot at the fighters from the settlements with his machine gun, picking them off like birds. The first thing the armistice committee had done was remove the sandbags, and indeed, they had rolled away the stones he'd used to mark Faris's grave. But if he looked closely, he could still tell—to within a hair's breadth—where Faris lay. He waited patiently before laying the gravestone, to see where the greedy fence's ambitions would end. And, when it was all over, and reams of barbed wire had gouged through his vineyards, he put up the gravestone and carved everything he had to say into the inscription. Then he fell silent. And sat on that low stool of his, with his eyes drawn to a horizon always looming with surprises, with no prayer beads in his hand.

"How was the harvest this year?" someone had asked, back when life was good.

Hajj Mohammed kissed his own hand front and back to show he was grateful for his blessings, a habit he'd inherited from his father, and his standard response to any question about his livelihood.

"You've grazed your hand, Hajj."

"Yes, I scraped it on the skimmer when I was stirring the juice."

And it wasn't just the skimmer that had scraped his hand. Even though he'd hired workers to trim the vines, mulch the land, and pick the grapes in his three vineyards—as well as all the vineyards that lay close to his village—Hajj Mohammed wasn't above working the land himself. He would fill his spacious lungs with the smell of the soil, refusing to remember that he was the village leader until the sun's red disc had sunk into the west. And at night, he would sit in his diwan, sharing out his coffee and listening to everyone who flocked there. When his prayer beads stopped clicking, it meant the evening was over, and that he was tired and longed for his bed in the loft, where he could lie back and fall asleep to the rustling of vines in the summer breeze.

"I hear production's reached five hundred cans?"

He wouldn't lie. But he didn't confess to the exact number, either. (This too, he had learned from his father—people's eyes burn hot with envy.) He'd try to find an answer that would allow him to avoid saying the number.

But he knew that five hundred cans wouldn't feel like such a big number if only he had a bigger press and more cauldrons. He began to think Faris hadn't just been idly philosophizing when he described the ideas that had filled his head as a student in Jerusalem. "Ya Abi," he'd said, "we can't keep making our molasses like this, the same way we've been doing for three generations. The world has moved on, and that mattock of yours is a joke compared to the tractors the settlers use. We need to start up a modern factory!"

He had nodded. With Faris, he was both weak and strong. But his son was asking a lot. He'd be lost without the trough, the cauldron, and the skimmer. And he wouldn't feel as proud as he did now when he inspected his cans, checking their soldering, and sticking the branded labels on them with his own hands:

Premium Molasses
Produced in the factories of Hajj Mohammed Etewi.

And underneath, in bigger letters:

Eat and Be Happy!

"Factories? You call that trough of yours a factory? You're fooling yourself, Abi."

"Don't be ungrateful for God's blessings, Faris. All our wealth comes from that trough."

"Of course, you're free to do as you wish, Abi. But I'll have to work somewhere else."

In the end, Hajj Mohammed had almost been convinced. In fact, he'd been completely convinced. He'd pondered over the best spot to build the factory… All it would cost him was his plans for a new hajj, the price of the half dozen spiral bracelets he would've bought for Umm Faris, and some jewelry he'd have bought for his daughters.

For Faris's sake, his only son among four daughters, he'd do anything. He'd even agree to take his name off the label and change with the times by making molasses in solid blocks, which he'd wrap in gilded paper like those Jews did in the settlement they'd built on the nearby plain.

But that fall, the state of the molasses—whether packed in a can or wrapped in gilded paper—had been the last thing on his mind. The wave of anger that swept the country had drowned out everything else. He had put down a deposit at the bank to secure the cost of new machines for the factory, but then he went and took the money back. Faris and his brothers-in-arms needed machine guns and ammunition, and they needed to set up barriers to face the cannons which had sprouted, like mushrooms, along the borders of the settlements. The diwan became a military headquarters, where members of the national guard would meet every night to share out weapons and duties. And all through that fall, and the winter that followed, Hajj Mohammed worried at his prayer beads with a nervousness he'd never shown before. But he needed to hide the anxiety his beads revealed, and to look confident when, in the third watch of the night, he went to check on the young men who crouched behind the barriers, their fingers frozen on the triggers. For the first time in his life, he forgot about the press and the cauldrons, and he didn't gather the cans or supervise their washing. He would travel once or twice a week to negotiate with committees from other cities for more ammunition. And when he and the committees had exhausted all their options, the barriers, in his eyes, became flimsy piles of cotton, and the men merely scarecrows in front of the armored cars that stole in under the cover of night to shoot and retreat.

And what a night it had been, that night when Faris lost his mind and crossed the barriers. He threw himself into the beam of a vicious spotlight, and then, like a madman, began to spray bullets at the armored vehicle. He made sure it keeled over, but it had already decorated his chest with ten bullets.

The car stopped, and Hajj Mohammed got out and looked at the village from a distance. The sun had begun to set, somewhat sluggishly, and the white houses seemed almost empty to him, draped in the shadow of a heavy stillness that left everything in a state of tired despair. But back home, before he reached out to remove the wooden beams that had secured the door while he was away, and before he took out his keys, he went to stand near the stone wall. The fence leaped out at him. It had eaten up half of the village's land and some of its houses, and stolen its natural extension into the plains that spread to the west, furrowed in patterns dictated by what would be planted. So this was what the fence had left to the village, and what it had left to him of his vineyards… The remains of the vines were heavy with fruit, the sweet-tart bunches twined in varying shades of yellow. But behind the fence, the vines were bare. They had hurried in to pick them clean, sweeping the harvest into the bellies of their trucks, where there was room for every kind of injustice. Turning quickly so a little boy crouched on a nearby rock wouldn't notice he was weeping, he soaked up his tears with the edge of his keffiyeh.

He went off to arrange for someone to put up the marble slabs, and the headstone and footstone; he'd had them made to keep the memory of Faris alive when the village remembered how it had paid for defeat with acts of heroism. A few days later, when the job was done, the men gathered round, talking about how the armistice had devastated them and stabbed its barbed wire into their eyes. But he merely nodded, his eyes fixed on the horizon. And he may or may not have seen how the vines drooped under the weight of bunches of grapes that dangled like cracked breasts because no one had lifted a hand to harvest them. The villagers had been waiting for him to come back and chew over his despair with them, but after he'd returned and finished building the grave, the days went by, and they didn't understand why he just sat there, letting his vines wither and dry out, and why, when they begged him to do something, he didn't answer, even to refuse. They too had suffered a great calamity, but as long as there was still life in them, they mustn't live as if they were already in their graves.

Then along came the clouds, leaning on the village's shoulder and waiting for a gust of wind to jostle them before pelting sheets of rain onto the vineyards. The grapevines were the first to suffer, and their stems were left blackened and bare. And people swore that Hajj Mohammed didn't taste a single one of his grapes, and he didn't let anyone else taste them, either. Some even swore they saw him ripping branches from the vines to feed the fire in his fireplace in winter—something no farmer would do, knowing full well that renewal is the miracle of life. Later, when the clouds had receded and warmth crept into the soil, the vines woke again, their tender green shoots stirring with life, and their leaves unfurling instinctively, like little flags. And when a hint of emotion seemed to glimmer in blank eyes, his friends found the courage to speak up and extracted two nods from him, a promise that he would do something this season. And they felt he wouldn't let them down when they saw him in the mornings, raising his dew-washed face to the sun and propping up fallen vines on a stake that he'd hammered into the ground. So, they reasoned, his faith had protected him, and the earth had awakened his ancient farmer's instincts. But, having understood all this, they still couldn't fathom why Hajj Mohammed was not only collecting all those bottles, but also paying whichever of the village boys that brought them to him one or two millimes for each.

Was it true… what Salman Abu Akef said? Was it true he…?

Could Salman Abu Akef be the smartest of them, and the quickest to figure out this mystery whose name, more than a year ago, had been Hajj Mohammed Etewi? The man who, simply put, was the village head and the best of its men, generous of hand and spirit, the heart and mind of their community?

Had Hajj Mohammed sold out?

The saintly man who had come from generations of molasses merchants, who was above reproach, who never missed a prayer or a day's fasting, and who had bought his ticket to the hereafter with seven rounds of hajj—would he do it?

But what was he doing with the bottles? Who could ease their suspicions and heal their heavy, grieving hearts? Those were his bottles; he didn't even bother to hide them. There were ever more of them, and the pile grew and grew until it could be seen by anyone looking behind his house into the backyard.

He had forsaken his pilgrimage and spent his piasters—and God knows they were rare these days—on empty bottles. And nobody knew what he would do with them, unless—astaghfirullah—he was planning to distill, making arak instead of molasses?

But Salman Abu Akef and the others didn't dare spell it out; they hadn't forgotten the night Hajj Mohammed had thrown Alyan the bus driver out of the diwan when he heard he'd been seen in a bar in Jerusalem, drinking a glass of arak with some used-car hawkers.

It was a riddle that kept the villagers' heads spinning all through that summer and fall. The answer seemed clear when he picked his grapes, down to the very last bunch, and didn't send out a single gift basket. He stored all the grapes in his house and left the trough and press untouched, buried under two years' worth of dust.

Had he sold out his hajj?

What more were they waiting for? Why didn't they say it out loud? Or make a song of it for the children—even the ones who'd pocketed his coins? They could sing it in rounds, one group chanting "Hajj Mohammed...," and the other replying, "...sold out his hajj."

Oh Hajj, you've fallen so low. And you don't even realize it because, ever since you picked your grapes, you have locked yourself out of sight.

They saw nothing of him for two months, except for fleeting glimpses when he made a quick trip to the grocer's and returned, just as quickly, to his house.

Two months. One season gave way to another, and the ground was covered in white. Winter, with its pounding winds, knocked on their doors, but they refused to open them.

Then one day they did.

That morning, a caravan of four boys—the same ones who had collected his bottles for him—went knocking on doors. Missing no one, they gave two or three bottles to everyone who appeared on the doorsteps.

They were a gift from Hajj Mohammed... filled to the brim. It was just as they'd expected, but with one small difference:

The bottles were filled with vinegar! And there was no new mystery to be solved. This time, no clever man, not even Salman Abu Akef, was needed to help them grasp the truth.

OUT OF TIME

BECAUSE HE LOVED THEM

When he woke that morning, he couldn't explain the feeling of foreboding that gripped him. He pressed his memory in the hopes of finding a reason in one of his dreams from the night before, but could recall nothing in particular. The dreams seemed muddled and confused, their beginnings and endings tangled together, and he was still feeling uneasy after he'd finished getting dressed. When he got on the bus, he found himself in no mood to speak to his colleagues, so he buried his head in a newspaper to keep their droning voices from reaching his ears. He didn't realize something was up until a hand reached out from behind to shake his shoulder, and a voice abruptly said, "Have you heard the news? They've arrested Wasfi."

For a moment, the bombshell that had just been dropped didn't penetrate his mind, and he started to look back at his paper, but the hand returned to shake him, and the voice returned to say, "You look like you don't believe it. *They've arrested Wasfi.*"

This time, he felt the newspaper slip from his fingers, and he barely knew what he was saying when he turned to the man behind him to ask, "Are you sure?"

"What do you think?"

Apart from him, the bus was carrying more than twenty other employees. The hum of their voices grew louder and their comments flew back and forth, silencing the chatty telephone operator who would watch a movie every day and then proceed, unprompted, to retell its story in agonizing detail. The comments ranged from fake displays of sympathy to gloating disguised as righteous indignation. As for him, he didn't know what to say. His heart beat faster, and the newspaper print swam in front of his eyes.

Eventually, the bus stopped in front of the relief agency, as it had done every morning for the past eleven years. He went in to take his place in the spacious office, conscious of the pointed looks sent his way by those who had arrived on an earlier bus; his close friendship with Wasfi forced them to be more guarded with their comments.

As he walked past one of them, he heard the man telling his colleague at the next desk that some employees had begun to smell very fishy. He swallowed the insult and sat down, trying to get a hold of himself as he checked the distribution lists, but his eyes passed over the names in a haze. When the office telephone rang, he felt at once that the call would be for him, and he got up to take it before being asked by the person nearest to the phone. He lifted the receiver with a trembling hand and listened as his manager, with no trace of emotion, asked to see him in his office. He didn't go back to put away his papers, but instead made his way to the door with twenty curious eyes fastened on him.

He walked down the corridor and knocked on his manager's door, pushing it open without waiting for an answer. With great effort, he forced a greeting from his lips and then stood in front of his manager, who didn't invite him to sit, but told him that suspicion had fallen on Wasfi over the recent embezzlements at the Third Distribution Center, leading to his arrest the day before. Because of his friendship with Wasfi, he was to appear in front of the agency's private investigator, who would ask him a few questions that might assist with the investigation. The manager hoped, he continued, that he would answer them honestly and objectively. He was to go directly to the investigator's office on the floor above.

The manager stopped talking, and he took the silence as an invitation to leave, so he nodded and walked out of the room. He made his way back through the long corridor and climbed the staircase's twenty steps, all while wondering why he felt so uneasy, as if this was all new to him. But hadn't he himself suspected Wasfi and tried to visit him when the embezzlements were discovered three days ago? He had failed to find him at home, even though he'd visited at different times of the night and day… He needed to get a grip on himself and be calm for his meeting with the investigator. Here was his office, the third on the right. The door was halfway open, so he went straight in.

The man looked at him questioningly. He had forgotten that the investigator knew the employees only by name, so he had to tell the man who he was.

"Oh, it's you. Sit."

He sat. And tried to look relaxed under the man's searching gaze. Remaining quiet, the man lit a cigarette from a pack, but didn't offer him one. He took two long drags without moving his eyes from him. The man's voice finally addressed him firmly. "Sorry to bother you, but I'm told you're a close friend of Wasfi's, the one who has been charged with embezzling from the distribution center—please don't interrupt. Yes, a charge of embezzlement. Maybe you can give us information that would help our enquiries. No, no—don't say anything before hearing my questions, perhaps there's nothing to defend."

The investigator stopped speaking for a moment. *Perhaps he's trying to choose his questions carefully. Should he, or should he not, tell him the truth?*

If he wanted to be truthful, he'd have to say, "Yes, I must admit I've noticed that Wasfi has been spending more than usual. He spent a hundred lira on a single evening at the nightclub! And when one of the performers took a shine to his gold lighter, he gave it to her willingly, just because she was a blonde. Yes, how could that not make him look guilty? I myself thought he was guilty. He always used to borrow money off me, and then, three months ago, he just stopped. I wasn't too shy to ask him about it. He claimed, as he flicked a speck of cigarette ash off his new suit, that his uncle—a building contractor in Kuwait—had started sending them money. But where was that uncle of his when he'd had to cut off his brother's education halfway through high school and get him a job as an office boy at a bank? I didn't buy the story about his uncle. And even though I pretended to believe it, my eyes gave me away. He became afraid of me. My friendship began to annoy him. He started to avoid going around in the same car as me, and he didn't include me in his evening outings. That contractor-uncle story was just a laughable, worn-out yarn."

Oh, the man's asking questions now. I should try to listen. Did I notice anything unusual about...? How could I have failed to notice? But why would I tell you all that? No, I won't tell. I can't take on that casual attitude of yours and toss out our friendship. It was a friendship of blood and bullets, of hunger and lost homes and wandering. He's no lowlife. Wasfi is not a lowlife. He nearly hit a doctor who wouldn't write a report to get a poor woman into the hospital after gangrene had almost eaten her leg off. And he's no thief. The small handouts he gives his widowed aunt and unemployed cousin come out of his salary first, before any other accounts are settled.

You weren't with us when we used to dream of a day when a miracle would send us to the border, and that we'd be driven there by a purpose more powerful than our miserable fates. You weren't with us when we collected donations for a magazine that would carry our nation's name and the weight of its worries. No, don't expect me to be frank, because I will never respect you, or love the truth as much as I love Wasfi—or as much as I've begun to hate him now, as I watch him turn into a thief. Wasfi's reckoning won't come at your hands, it'll be between me and him. As for you, I can only defend him in front of you. Don't accuse me with your eyes. All I have to say is, "I've known Wasfi since he was a child. We were students together and we worked together. It's not easy for me to believe he would stoop so low."

My God, what a bitter pill you're forcing down my throat when you say, with your foreign wisdom: "My friend, in circumstances like yours, who knows when anyone might be driven to become a thief?"

The investigator shifted in his swivel chair, indicating that he should leave, so he got up, feeling the blood in his body pushing in a sudden mad rush to his head, as if he'd broken out in a fever that was eating away at him, reaching the very ends of his hair. He went back the way he came, somehow managing to stumble his way down the stairs to his office. When he walked into the room, heads lifted inquiringly from the papers that sat in front of them, but they soon bent down again when faced with his angry red eyes.

The distribution lists were still waiting, countless names with no beginning and no end, a caravan of lost souls waiting for him to dole out their daily bread. He grabbed the papers and mindlessly tore them up, throwing the pieces into the bin and then cradling his head in his hands as he tried to ease the sting of the words that buzzed around in it.

"Who knows when anyone might be driven to become a thief." That man... What he'd said was no lie. And although the investigator had been stony-faced—those people were too sly to show emotions of any kind—he wished *he* could say those words himself, just as cleverly, and that he could add, "or a criminal or a lowlife or a whore!"

Yes, he would watch his people fall, one after the other, when that "moment" imposed itself. He got up from his desk, sat back down, then got up again and walked to the window, where he smiled pityingly at a fig tree in a nearby garden. Winter had left its stiff, dry branches bare, and it looked like a twisted skeleton whose limbs were long dead. With his eyes on the tree, he smoked three cigarettes while his thoughts blazed ahead at such speed that he grew tired of keeping up with them.

He threw his third cigarette out the window and went back to his desk. Something had sprouted in his head that looked nothing like those branches. Something which, if it flourished, would eat away all the dryness. He looked around for someone who could think out loud with him, but of all the faces scattered in every corner of the big room, there wasn't a single one he felt comfortable with. He reached into the drawer, looking for a pen, because he had to say something before leaving this place and never coming back.

What should he write? Should he tell the story of the brother who had become a thief? It was common knowledge now. And every one of these people would chew it over with his family at the table, not realizing that he himself, in the eyes of the investigator, was a potential thief.

So let him instead tell the stories he had come to know during his long days at work: the stories of the criminal, the whore, and the sonofabitch.

Fayyad Al-Hajj Ali used to be a farmer in one of the villages up north. When he was drunk, he would say the grain in his field was as tall as a man, although, if he described it before he'd gulped down half a bottle of arak, neat, with no water, then it reached no higher than a man's waist. In our country, his land was always green because our sky was generous and our soil forgiving, and our arms were neither idle nor weak.

When the land went, the only thing that remained of the harvests was the image he had of the grain that was sometimes as tall as a man, and other times only reached his waist. He became one of those hundreds whose hunger was almost never sated as long as there was more for them to eat, and whose sole comfort—once they got tired of stuffing their faces—was in getting their women pregnant.

He came to the refugee camp with a wife and one child and, by the end of eleven years, the card he presented at the start of each month showed he was supporting a wife and five children.

On distribution days, he was always first to arrive, holding out his card and taking the rations: flour, margarine, worm-ridden dates, and dried beans that were more chaff than grain. He was one of the few who didn't lose their tempers, or swear at me, or hold me entirely responsible for the weevils eating away at their bread.

Once, about a year ago, he came up to me, carrying the humble card in one hand and a gunny sack in the other. My assistant hadn't yet started to measure out his share when a woman with a swollen belly walked into the center. She grabbed my sleeve and kissed my hand, begging me, in tears, not to hand over the rations to that lowlife because he would sell them at the door and get drunk with the price of them, leaving his wife and children to starve for the whole month. Before the woman had finished speaking, her husband had turned on her like a vicious wolf, and her red eyes widened in fear. He laid into her with his fists and feet, punching and kicking while my assistant and I tried in vain to hold him back.

The woman dropped to the ground, her blood rushing out, staining the edges of the flour sacks. And when I called the agency to summon an ambulance and it came time to transfer the patient, the hospital refused to admit her without a report from the agency's doctor. Before I had time to find the doctor and get the report, the woman had lost too much blood, and all that was left was her swollen, waxen body.

She didn't last long at the hospital: by midday she was dead.

Fayyad Al-Hajj Ali wasn't a criminal.

He used to be a kind-hearted farmer, but he lost his dignity when he lost his land. That's what one of the old men at the camp said; he told me that, back then, Fayyad had been gentleness itself, and that his father had slaughtered five sheep when he married him off to his beloved cousin.

I don't know what happened to Fayyad's children because they left to live with their uncle in another camp, but I can confirm two truths: their ration card now gives them supplies for five people instead of seven, and Fayyad is serving a sentence of fifteen years of hard labor. And if Fayyad, as he strikes his pickaxe on the roadworks, were to talk to the other inmates about his crops, he'd say—since there's no alcohol in there—that the grain was only half as tall as a man, and that his land was always green, because the soil was forgiving and the sky was generous and the men's arms were never idle or weak.

And I've met the whore.
No, don't look for her name in the torn-up distribution lists; I know her from somewhere else, and her new name is not the one she had in her country.
At the end of each month, clutching what was left of our salary, which we'd struggled to split between rent, groceries, and school fees, we used to try to forget that we were miserable by getting drunk. And when we were drunk, our footsteps would take us in search of one of those places where red lights beckoned, oozing with sin.
Once, Wasfi was with me. He went in first— everything comes in turn, that's what we tell the people we give rations to—but soon came out again. He was pale and trembling, and he dragged me by the arm out into the street. When I tried to object to this rude treatment, he nearly broke down crying. "Do you remember Ahmed, our trainer back when we were in the guard?" he asked. "Remember that day when he was killed in a Jewish raid at the edge of town, and his friends brought us back his body? And we refused to wash him because he was martyred, so we buried him covered in blood after mourning him with a hundred poems and speeches, and swearing to take a thousand heads in return for his? Do you remember? Well, I saw a picture of him in there, the same one we used for the funeral flyers; it was hanging off the corner of a broken mirror. I stared at that picture and froze. And when I finally turned to face the woman, I didn't dare ask. She had the same chin, the same fine upturned nose… My desire dried up as I held the picture, and I put it back in its place and walked to the door. She followed me and spoke in a trembling voice, as if to apologize for this bitter ending.
"We had no one but him to rely on. And when my mother died while we were in exile, this was the only path left for me to take."
Wasfi and I walked along in silence; the effects of the drinks we'd downed quickly dissipated, and a feeling of loss squeezed our hearts. And from that day on, we began to fear those houses that were lit by lanterns dripping with sin—some of our own sisters might have ended up there if the Jewish fighters' bullets hadn't missed us.

And I've met the sonofabitch, too.

Who would it be, if not Abu Saleem?

His tent is the biggest in the camp, and he's added three smaller ones to it. He can always be found in front of the big tent's door, next to a wooden cart piled high with all sorts of goods, which he sells to the refugees at any price he wants.

Unlike his neighbors, Abu Saleem isn't poor. He used to have a job at the port and still gets a pension from the Mandate government. Plus, two of his sons work in Kuwait and have never stopped supporting him. His wife's arms are loaded with gold spiral bangles and he's rich enough to lend his neighbors money at rates of fifty or sixty percent.

Abu Saleem is the camp spy; he's the first to track a refugee's every movement and the first to tell the agency when someone dies so it can cancel their rations immediately. But he himself—and we don't know how—collects rations for his sons in Kuwait and his mother who died five years ago.

A big tent called "the school" stands at the center of the camp. More than a hundred children are crammed into it, where they're taught by an ancient schoolmaster, a relic from the Ministry of Education in Palestine whose eyes can barely read what his hand writes on the worn-out blackboard.

In winter, rain leaks in from big holes in the tent, turning the ground into a muddy sludge. It's impossible for the children to sit cross-legged on damp mats in the mud, so the school goes on a break that lasts for as long as a merciful God keeps watering the fields and livestock without reserve.

The camp residents complained to me about this misery known as a school, so I suggested that they raise a petition and threaten to keep their children away from that filthy sty until the agency built them a new one from stone.

They tried to get the teacher to write the petition, but he was too scared to do it, so I volunteered to write it myself. Barely three days later, I received a warning from the agency, instructing me not to interfere in matters that didn't concern me—my mission started and ended with the distribution center.

I never doubted that Abu Saleem was the source of the "intelligence," and the school went on being a tent with knowledge pouring out of its holes.

The worn-out teacher also remained, and when he got tired, there were five prefects to teach in his place; they disciplined his students with a stick, which, in his opinion, was by far the most useful means of correction.

The only thing that changed at the camp was that Abu Saleem bought a television set; he put it up in the front section of his big tent and fixed the aerial onto the tent pole. He charged an entrance fee for whoever wanted to watch it: a quarter of a lira for adults and ten piasters for children, and woe betide anyone who tried to peek in through the holes in the tent.

Yes, I know each and every one of them.
The thief, the criminal, the whore, and the sonofabitch.
And they're no worse than anyone else. They tried to find themselves identities that would set them apart from the herd, which had been reduced to mere numbers in the lists, growing with every birth and shrinking with every death. Half the herd was spitting up blood, and everyone who belonged to it had been stripped of the power to reject anything.

No, you didn't lie, Investigator, when you said, "My friend, in circumstances like yours, who knows when anyone might be driven to become a thief?"

And tomorrow, when you read my words and I am in another place, please don't consider them an apology. I did it because I don't want to become a thief, or to live forever a traitor who feeds his people rocks to suppress their despair by way of their stomachs.

The ghost who ambled leisurely in the light drizzle that washed the street seemed no more than a loiterer, someone who couldn't muster the enthusiasm to go home after a dull evening in a café. The half-blind lights' reflections in the small puddles lent a little color to the dark desolate street, but did nothing to expose the flushed face that burned with a feverish glow.

Nothing broke the sound of night except the cries of a sleepless, willful rooster who didn't care when he crowed, even on a night when the moon had died, and the dry cough of a watchman whose chest rattled with cheap tobacco.

People had gone to sleep, holding their worries close, and leaving him to face the world on his own with the flat bottle that he'd filled with gasoline and hidden in his back pocket, and a box of matches that he'd paired with a lighter, in case the matchsticks let him down.

His heavy footsteps knew where they were going; they slowed down only to ward off any suspicion that might attach itself to feet hurrying through a sleeping neighborhood.

Before stopping at the door of the distribution center, the ghost headed, seemingly casually, toward the watchman. He gave the man an offhand greeting that he hoped would pave the way for a throwaway conversation and allow him the chance to offer the man a cigarette.

The watchman received the greeting kindly and, when the passerby lingered, said that the night was warm despite the rain, but its warmth didn't make it any shorter, and he cursed his job, which turned other people's night into his day.

And when he heard a sympathetic answer, he didn't refuse the cigarette the man offered him; he sucked it down till the last breath before realizing the face in front of him was that of a stranger to the neighborhood, since he knew all the faces here, one and all. But that meant nothing; the nights were never free of loiterers, and this one had been good company. He wished the stranger could stay a little longer so he would have someone to listen to him, instead of having to talk to himself. But the other man soon resumed his shuffling walk, not bothering to avoid the potholes full of rainwater, or to shelter from the drizzle that hadn't let up since the early hours of the night. The road curved to one side and swallowed him up, and the watchman had the street to himself again.

But he didn't have the street to himself. From behind the curve, a head quickly looked out and disappeared, then came out again. Gleaming, eager eyes searched for signs of the heaviness that grew in the watchman's head, watching him as a delicious numbness spread to his limbs and head, and he struggled to sit down on the short-legged chair that he kept under a low balcony so he could shelter from the rain whenever it grew stronger. He dropped his body down onto the chair, with his shotgun across his knees, and his head was soon drooping into a sleep that he couldn't fight off—after all, sleep rules everyone, even watchmen.

The stranger lurking behind the curve roused himself and groped for the key to the center that the man carried with him, laughing at the irony that had turned him into an outlaw, like the ones whose stories were made into countless films. His footsteps were light as he headed for the door and gently opened it, avoiding any squeaks so the drugged watchman wouldn't wake up and ruin the adventure that was burning away at his heart.

He pushed the door shut, using the key to lock it behind him. Nobody knew the ins and outs of this warehouse like he did, and he reached out confidently to feel for the light switch.

Light flooded the place and disturbed the feasting rats, who grew fatter and more immune to the red poison pellets by the day. Even the rats took liberties with the refugees' property, but their thievery ended with the needs of their bellies. If only Wasfi was as honorable as those rats… The jest would surely make Wasfi laugh in his cell if he heard it. He'd tell him tomorrow when they met, the thief and the… what? What name would he carry tomorrow? The agency hadn't come across a case like his before. It had known thieves and bribe-takers, blue-eyed activists who preached humanitarianism for more than a thousand dollars a month, and know-it-alls who claimed that politics stopped at the agency's door—so what names would they choose for him tomorrow?

It was a question he couldn't dwell on for long; he had to choose a spot for the fire. And he needed to collect some empty sacks and pour gasoline over them from the bottle he was carrying, then let the flames devour all this food. Beans, flour, dates, and raisins: a feast fueled by humiliation... *Oh, why was he dragging his feet? Was he afraid the watchman would wake up and that he'd be arrested for stealing, and then no one would ever acknowledge him as anything but a thief?*

He hurried to collect the sacks, stacking them one on top of the other and pouring every last drop of gasoline onto them before throwing the empty bottle at the far wall, where it splintered. Next, he lit a match and brought it to the edge of one of the sacks, holding the lighter to the other side. The sack sucked the fire in, and the flames spread through it from both ends, soon drawing closer to each other, then mixing and embracing. Leaving the sacks, he went to bring the jars of fat closer, then scraped out a few lumps from them, throwing them onto the pile. He went round to the other side, smeared fat onto a few more sacks, and fed them a spark from a match. His fire flourished and blossomed, singeing his dark skin with its heat and making his blood run hot in his veins. A savage elation came over him, prompting him to take his knife and slash the bellies of the bloated sacks. Their contents scattered at his feet and he trod all over them with lurching steps. He took pleasure in laughing as he imagined the foul-mouthed swearing mob tearing at his skin with their nails and burying him under their curses.

Calm down, I have things to say tomorrow when I'm taken—when I take myself—to the police station. So don't throw your stones at this despicable man whose sins have outshone the sins of the thief, the criminal, the sonofabitch, and the whore.

Save your stones and grope in the ashes of my fire for your new life. Look at me threshing your flour with my shoes and soiling my feet with the dust from your beans. I'm teaching you to go hungry so your despair will rise up and rebel, so you can grow, grow beyond the grip of a humble loaf of bread.

When he got to the door, he leaned his back against it, his burning eyes drinking in the sight of the wild, ravenous flames. He felt for his cigarettes with a shaking hand, remembering the watchman's cigarette with a smile. What would the watchman say to the authorities tomorrow, when the center had become a blackened lump of coal? That it was an accident, the hand of fate? It may have been fate, but it was shaped by human hands!

The tongues of fire rose higher, and the flames began to roast him, their crackling now audible as they came closer to the edge of the only window in the eastern wall. The fire would eat away the wood and melt the iron, and then a blazing portal would open out onto the night, lighting up a new path. And everyone would know—all the refugees, everyone at the agency, and the investigator in particular—that he was something bigger than a thief and better than a sonofabitch, and that his people would not curse him if they went hungry. After all, he'd only burned their food, and let his fire loose over the spoils of rats and thieves because… because he loved them!

ACKNOWLEDGMENTS

Heartfelt thanks to my publisher and editor Marcia Lynx Qualey for taking a chance on me and allowing me time to learn on the job, for her nuanced and inspired editing, and for making the entire process of producing this book an utter joy. Thanks also to Leonie Rau for her meticulous proofreading and to Hassân Almohtasib for the beautiful cover.

    A huge thank you to the members of the Bristol Translates Arabic group, the Arabic Literary Translators groups, the Levantine Arabic Dialects group, the Early Birds group, Rania Issa and to my mother, Asma El-Gazzar, for always being ready to help with translation conundrums. I'd also like to thank Bahaa Kadamani, Managing Director of Grapeful, Lebanon, for his willingness to help a total stranger find the definition of a utensil used in producing grape molasses. And I will be forever grateful to Hossam Abouzahr for his invaluable Living Arabic dictionary, which gives definitions and examples in both Classical Arabic and dialects.

    Out of Time is my first book-length project and the culmination of a somewhat unintentional journey to literary translation. I've been touched and humbled by the support and kindness of so many people along the way. Yvette Judge and Isobel Abulhoul's comments on my early attempts were the spark that set me off on this path. Michael Cooperson and Neil Hewison generously gave me advice about the field and encouraged me to give it a go. Marcia Lynx Qualey and Sawad Hussain have gone out of their way to help me at every opportunity—I cannot thank them enough. And Flora Rees has been there for me from the beginning, providing wisdom, reassurance, and brilliant editing from which I always learn so much.

    To my husband and sons, my parents and my sister, thank you for your love and encouragement, and for putting up with me going on endlessly about tricky bits that were giving me grief.

ABOUT THE AUTHOR

Samira Azzam was born in Acre, Palestine in 1927. After completing her basic education, she found work as a schoolteacher at 16, and was later appointed headmistress of a girls' school. She was still in her teens when her stories began to appear in the journal *Falastin* under the pen name Fatat al-Sahel, or Girl of the Coast. When Azzam and her family were forced to flee Palestine in 1948, they went first to Lebanon; in the years that followed, Azzam would work as a journalist around the region. Azzam was also an acclaimed translator, bringing English-language classics into Arabic as she published the stories that have since appeared in five collections. In her brief life, she translated works by Pearl Buck, Sinclair Lewis, Somerset Maugham, Bernard Shaw, John Steinbeck, Edith Wharton, and others.

ABOUT THE TRANSLATOR

Ranya Abdelrahman is a translator of Arabic literature into English. After working for more than 16 years in the information technology industry, she changed careers to pursue her passion for books, promoting reading and translation. She has published translations in *ArabLit Quarterly* and *The Common*.